It Rarely Happens

It Rarely Happens

Aamir Sohail Akhtar

PARTRIDGE
A Penguin Random House Company

To order additional copies of this book, contact
Partridge India
000 800 10062 62
orders.india@partridgepublishing.com

www.partridgepublishing.com/india

ABOUT THE AUTHOR

Aamir Sohail Akhtar was born in a small district of Bihar in a very humble family. He is pursuing his B.Tech from a well-reputed college in Delhi. He was in his third year of B.Tech when his book was getting published. He always thought to do different, so giving an edge to writing, he has given his imagination—the word to express in his book.

CONTENTS

ACKNOWLEDGEMENT

All the thanks to the Almighty God for his blessings.

To parents, family and Harsha – the centre of my happiness. There are many who lived their lives and ended up knowingly or unknowingly contributing to the book.

My father who provided me the initial kick and further motivated by 'Harsha' and all the hard work done by my friend 'Omer'.

May be many are in state of shock upon knowing that we can write and worse – getting published.

Thanks to the Partridge to consider my good work and a very hearty thanks to 'Mr. Maveric Pana' who always inspired me and never let me down.

All my friends and batch-mate who always supported me with my work and often providing me proxy attendance when needed.

My family who constantly supported me whether it were my parents or sisters.

My friend encouraged me a lot specially 'Harsha' and ofcourse Omer without whom I wont be able to finish the writing.

Fortunate enough and glad to have all such support when required a lot.

With all my heart I thank to everyone who surrounded me the whole time to wind up myself and motivated and pushed me to go for something different.

"I DADICATED THIS BOOK TO MY MOTHER AND FATHER WHO SHAPED MY CAREER, MY SISTER FOR HER UNCONDITIONAL LOVE FOR ME."

PROLOGUE

As soon as she replied Yes to me she went away from the class out of shyness and didn't want to face me any more right there.

She left and all the girls present there were smiling at me as if I had won a battle and they were there to welcome me with a smile. One of them was so happy and excited as if she had received the question paper before the exam…!!!

For me it was just like any dream that I proposed any girl for the first ever time and it got accepted. I was like in the seventh world, it seemed like everything had stopped for a moment I was continuously staring at the gate from where Tamannah left the class. My friends too were standing over there but I couldn't find a sight of them. I was just lost.

My all friends were calling me to come out of the class but I couldn't even hear them nor could I see them. For me I was still at that moment when Tamannah was at the gate with a shying smile on her face, keeping her head down and moving out by escaping from her friends. Everything slowed down slowly and I could grab each and every moment and captured it in my eyes.

START

It was a bright sunny day in the school when I first saw her. I was just startled seeing her; I didn't know how to respond to the situation to such external stimuli. To be very honest, I had never seen a girl as pretty as she was. She was in her school suit as unexpected to be worn by any of our school girl. Only a handful of girls dared to wear so, because such girls are often not appreciated and talked by many. They are considered to be the person not able to interact with the path of high society people as they are. But I always wanted girls to wear Indian dress for what they are made of.

I always like those girls who love to go for suit. She was in an INDIAN look and I fell in love with her in the very first slight contact of my eyes for just a shake. I didn't know that, was it her dress which attracted me or it was attraction towards her shyness or may be her dress, I was just confused, which perfectly reflected the charm of her face, her cuteness, her innocence etc, etc, etc and many more. I didn't know the reason but its effect could be clearly seen on my face.

Till then I didn't know which class she really belonged to. Was she my senior? Or my junior!! If later is the case then it would be easy for me to atleast stare at her without any fear of being noticed. I could easily go a step ahead and talk to her. But doing this too will need all of my courage and ofcourse ability to attract her in my first attempt as I had never did it before. But if earlier is the case then I had to be very cautious as many from our senior will surely try to do friendship with her. I asked Sahil, my fast friend from same class and same school about her but he too didn't know anything about her. He only told that she joined the school two days earlier itself and unfortunately I was absent both of the days.

This taught me a lesson that if you have to search for a girl then you have to be punctual and be daily visitor to school. We all know happiness comes in small packages and it was for me which I missed initially. My mind was wandering here and there in more than a hundred question only related to her but suddenly the assembly bell rang and we all had to hurry up to make our line according to our class.

I was somewhere in the middle of the line talking to my friend facing the girls and suddenly I felt someone throwing the atom bomb of Hiroshima and Nagasaki into my place but I was stuck there without any pain. It was such a kind of atom bomb which I would love to bear happily everytime.

I was surprised and astonished to see her standing in the girl's row of my class. Yes, she too was a student of class 9 and luckily my batch-mate. I was so excited and happy that I could give my whole money if someone asked me. Money, that times meant a reason to smile, a reason to be superior but I could have given that too for her.

In the whole assembly I was thinking how to talk to her, what to do for friendship and all other stupid things. Very happily I went to the class after assembly with thousands of blooming dreams in my mind. I sat quietly but was very anxious to know her name. There was nothing to distract me from seeing her. From the very first interaction I was totally in her grip if ever she asked me my life I would have given it to her very happily without knowing her name.

'Name!! I don't need to know her name as I had wondered a million of her name and kept a secret lovely name for her, "CUTIE". Yes, it perfectly defined her cuteness and ofcourse my love for her.' Seeing her I was fully hypnotized, I couldn't see anything except her. Up till now I only knew that she is the one I was waiting for.

Let me introduce her complexion. She is a girl with a perfectly toned body. She was fairer than anyone in the class with an attractive slim body and hopefully she was in suit which I liked the most about her. She looked stunning in her black and white suit.

In this single hour I was being noticed by almost every person of my class but I didn't know that, as I was out of the world on the ninth cloud just by seeing her. I was thinking what a lucky man was I to have her as my class mate.

I was a big fool. How could I forget, I am not the single one studying in the class but a whole group of sixty student and might be possible for many others to think somewhat similar but not exactly those of mine.

I was damn sure that no one there was having the same or as much feeling for her as I had and all I knew because of my good interaction with whole class. I knew how my classmates think about a girl. They saw them with their mouth widened to engulf them if ever they get any chance. "Everyone should have girls but only to entertain and play with them" according to guys.

Its wrong here to tell that whole class was like that, there were some really honest, brilliant and single girl stand type friend too but there numbers were too limited to count. The rest students didn't have much reputation for girls but I had, and all this because of my mom who always taught me to have respect for every one especially girls and women as they were the real person to be respected and these words of my mom stuck in my pea-sized brain forever and I really don't know how this miracle did happen.

It was truly a miracle for me. I was always surrounded by the people of various thoughts and feelings, each one of them had their own philosophy and hypothesis towards life and girls, specially the later one. I had to listen all the fucking shit they vomit with all the friends and, in all that type of circumstances I was left untouched with their thoughts. Thanks to my mom who always uttered such 'pravachan' due to which I had a truly pure feeling for her.

Slap! A hard hit on my head from behind!

"Who the f*****g shit is that?" I screamed as much louder as I could.

All my friends were smiling facing me. "What was that?" I asked.

Beta tu to gaya kaam se. ladki ka chakkar bahut kharab hota hai. kutta paal le par ladki mat paal. Sahil opened his mouth.

"What are you all talking about bro. Ladkiii.? Whooo.? I.?"

Zyada teez mat ban saale sab samajh me bhi aa raha hai aur dikh bhi raha hai. Sahil again

"No bro! You have mistaken me. I am not getting involved with any girls. Really, trust me!! And if ever this happened then you all my friends will be the one whom I personally would tell at first." I tried to handle the situation.

To tu saale usko baar baar ghoor kyun raha hai. aur bhi log hai dekhne ko lekin usi ko kyun dekh raha hai. Rajveer.

"Whom!! That girl?"

haan bete wahi. Rajveer.

"Oh! She is the new comer, friends and I am just seeing her first time so a little astonished." I thought the conversation to end here after my explanation but more punches were waiting for me.

first time? saale assembly se pahle kon puch raha tha iske baare me. Sahil opened his fucking mouth and I really wanted to piss on him right there.

I meant what the need for him to open his big boasting mouth, can't he swallow it for me or if he did want to tell then why in public with all four of us (I, SAHIL, RAJVEER, AAKASH) present there.

"No friend, nothing's like that."

jaane de ise, ab kabhi use dekhe to batata hoon. Aakash.

I had to be very careful after being threatened by Aakash and all my dumbo friends. I had to be much more cautious about my where-about. If I had to see her then it was going to be too hard for me to steal my eyes from all my idiots friends who from then onwards looked for me to make fun. Moreover if they wanted they could hit me at any time without any prior reason, that's how a friend behaves.

I always ignore there stupidity which they usually do but it is not apt to say that I hate them. I love them really being my friend and there notorious act which make whole class burst into laughter. All of them has its own specialty and privilege.

Rajveer was having good vocal sound therefore he imitated almost every song and often he creates his own song out of one in the market by simply shifting the line or changing some word. His favorite created edited song was :

kala-kala rang hai tera,
ujle-ujle baal,
ek tuhi kangaal hai gori,
baki sab dhanwaan.

We all enjoyed his company not only due to his editing ability but also because of his vast collection of jokes of many types.

Sahil was typical Indian guys who never lost a chance to have fun and make a fun of others, and his easy prey, were girls. He always used to tease them but we had really nice, cooperative girls in class who never minded and enjoyed thoroughly with us. Sahil was good at his studies too, so he always had an upper hand from many others in the class.

Aakash was a guy, who really was a guy (cow) by nature, he not even a single time tried to do any unfair means to any. His nature was superb, he didn't hurt anyone. He, all the time stayed with us to have fun by noticing our activity and our deeds towards others.

At last let me introduce myself. My name is Lucky and I was always considered to be the bright student among the teacher and my classmate from my childhood, but being involved in notorious activities I was scolded in front of my teacher and classmate by my lovely mom everytime I went with her to attend parent - teachers meeting in the school, rather being praised for my result. My feedback given by my teacher seemed to overshadow my result by mom and that's the reason I always preferred to go along with my father for every parent -teachers meeting, as my father never scolded me and neither he told those feedbacks to my mom and so a double gain type situation gets created.

"No scolding by mom and good image in class". But my father was rarely available for such meetings. As far as I remember not more than five times in my whole school life, my father was there with me and in a year atleast six meetings were to be attended, so every time I had to go with my mom. I don't know, why she did so infront of all and if this, then why at home? I always believed the school situation to be the trailer and I knew that the whole picture of not less than three hours is waiting for me after reaching at home and then the much awaited things get started.

My Mom took the turn to make me understand to behave sincerely with the classmates and as usual I said yes to mom. She threatened me not to have such feedback in future, but I knew that this was happening from my 1st standard itself and now I was in 9th, I have been getting such appreciation from consecutive nine years without any break, then why to break my own record for just one year.

My mom was too clever, she herself came to school to pay the fees on time, and everytime she met my principal, my class-teacher and working women whom we used to call 'Bua-ji' and got enquired about me. Everytime I told her to give me the money to submit in school, but she denied.

Now the good thing was that my CUTIE was sitting on the bench in the other row exactly opposite to me, because of which I could see her by being little cautious.

The next teacher entered the class and after a few words for us he turned to her.

"New comer?", asked Sir to my CYTIE.

"YES, SIR." replied CUTIE.

"What's your name?" he questioned again.

Let me tell you, I was waiting for only this question to be asked and wanted to know her name very badly.

"Tamannah!!", she replied in a low voice.

Some more questions were asked but I didn't give much attention to them as my whole attention was to know her name only.

TAMANNAH!! What a nice name it was!

Chanting her name a hundred times and singing the song having same name (tumse milne ki tamanna hai, pyaar ka irada hai...) surpassed my wholen day. I was always thinking about to how to talk to her but didn't get any way, in the planning itself to talk to her, one week passed away.

Next very day as I entered the school gate I saw Sahil standing there waiting for me, as I reached nearer to him, he said, `guess what?` I really didn't understand what happened to him, but something good for sure as he asked that without shaking his hands with me which was very unusual at first sight. After my negligence he himself told me

`Two hottest girls have arrived in school and fortunately both of them are in 9`[th] `standard.`

"Both of them are damn hot bro." Sahil said in his exciting voice.

"Whatever, I don't care, and by the way you are telling this to me! Can't you remember the day a week back when you all were making fun of me only by just staring to a new comer?"

"Oh! Bro, forget the past and live in present dear." Sahil said,

"No, how could I forget that, if you can do that to me then why cant me?

"O my friend! Forget that, it was just a fun." Sahil.

I really wanted so because it will not only permit me to stare at my CUTIE but also I was sure, they are gonna help me handling the situation, but not at all in a single go. I wanted myself to be convinced hard by him, so, I pretended to be a little angry.

"Ok! Fine, come to class and let me keep my bag first."

I wasn't moved even a bit by his description for those girls. I was fully determined that my CUTIE would be far better than those girls, and in fact the whole girls, not only in school but also in the whole world. I was so much attached with her that I knew that no one is better than her even by an ounce. I knew that if such was the situation without any conversation then what would happen if she spoke to me, I would go dumb-stuck.

For me she was the most beautiful girl and no one would occupy her place in my heart. She meant every thing to me. I didn't know she love me or not or I even didn't know that she had seen me or recognized, or noticed me as her classmate or not, but one thing I knew was that, I loved her from the core of my heart and I would always love her till my last breath. She is the only one I love and wish to live with, I love to die with, I love to do anything she asked for, love to do anything for her little cute smile to appear on her face.

We went to class and I saw two new girls.

"She is the one I was talking about." Sahil said pointing towards the new girls in the class.

"How does she look?" Sahil added.

"Yes, nice choice!" I

I was thinking if these girls are thought to be nice looking and hot then my CUTIE would surely be called as a mix-up of sun and moon, 'Sun for the hotness and Moon for her astonishing, charming beauty'. Those girls were good, but not so good enough to be called the hottest.

Sahil went mad on one of them. He was on the top and I thought it to be a good sign for me to go a step further and talk to my CUTIE without any fear of being caught or noticed, then if my friends even saw me doing that then they would give their consent, but, one great problem was friend 'Rajveer' who had to be taken into consideration. Till then he didn't like any girl but if he too started liking someone then my problem would be over forever or if not then I had to convince him for my deep blooming love for my CUTIE and he would surely agree to help.

I knew how to handle my friends, its true that they are always in the mood for some mischief but after-all they were my friends and were always ready to help.

I didn't have to bother for Sahil as he already went flat on the new comer girl, it would be quite easy for me to tackle him, as from then he would be in my grip. The names of both the new girls whom Sahil thought to be the hottest were 'Insha' and 'Ruksar' and he liked Ruksar, chanting her name as if it was some holy mantras and some baba had told him to do so a million times in a day inorder he wished to make her his soul-mate.

Soul-mate? He can never have a soul-mate because he always kept the girls in his sole. He had a very famous quotation of use and throws and always seemed to follow that, he was always in search of some new hottie and it didn't matter for him whether he was in school, coaching, party or on road. He was very hopeful and always had a condom in his purse and the reason he often tells;

Insan ko hamesha aashavadi hona chahiye kya pata kis mod pe iski zaroorat pad jaye aur main in sab ke liye hamesha taiyyar rahta hoon.

Things were going nicely all these days but I didn't get any opportunity to have a talk with her but in these fifteen to twenty days all of my classmates had very truly understood my feeling for her and specially the girls, as it was very logical too.

I mean she always sat beside her friend in the girl's row and everytime I saw her. So very possibility to be noticed, I used to see her more than a hundred times in a day and while doing so a handful of times our eyes got contacted and as soon as our eye met I quickly start seeing some other side as if I was surveying the class, and very eagerly and happily start narrating the scene to my friends, ''She saw me yaar. Our eyes got contacted". After saying this, my friend oftenly saw her and said;

```
jhut bol raha hai. wo to dusri taraf
dekh rahi hai. phekta hai saale. Rajveer.
```

I never understand why every friend needs verification in other's love. If someone had to tell something then he must have to verify it, otherwise you will be a liar, pheku and many more.

In my case too, I was nothing without proof, no matter how old our friendship was. Proof on hand and you will be on the top. But how could I give them the proof of my truth, she hardly knew me and what to tell to her that 'you please stare at me for a minute and I would let my friend see it and then they are gonna believe my words'. So disgusting and irritating!!

Till now each one from my class knew that I love her except her. This is the basic difference between the love of a boy and that of a girl.

'If a girl loves a boy then no one knows except the girl. But if a boy loves a girl then everyone knows except the girl.'

In these few days Sahil really went mad on Ruksar and Rajveer too was taking somewhat interest in girls and both of it was good for me. During lunch break I was talking to my friend named Palak and suddenly she asked me the toughest question.

"Do you really love Tamannah?" Palak asked me.

My face went red like a tomato due to shyness, my head was down and there was slight shying smile on my face.

"Don't feel shy Lucky." She forced me to answer question.

I could only blush at her bold question and didn't know what to answer. I knew every one was aware of my love but I never expected such question so early and obviously not from a girl. I know my love was pure and true so I decided not to keep it a secret.

"Yes, I love her!!" I replied quite boldly after shyin a little.

"Wow! That's great." Palak jumped out in joy.

"Is she aware of my feeling?" I enquired after seeing a positive response from her.

"Not really! But she should know it. Sometimes she notices you incessantly seeing her." Palak responded.

"Does she say anything about me?" I queried as I was having number of questions related to her running in my mind.

"No, she only said that you very often see her and many a time your eye gets contacted and when it happens so you pretend to see somewhere else and didn't keep contact for long." Palak replied.

I smiled a little which reflected my shyness and worry too.

"You don't worry. She will get to know about your love very soon and we all will do it for you." She further added.

This is what a girl can do if she is your good friend and such friends are very much required in the current situation as of mine.

I always had a good understanding with girls of my class. Due to my good friendship with almost all girls, many of my classmates felt offended and a little annoyed, some might have the feeling of jealousness but I didn't care.

Now I was aware that she too has started noticing my behavior as stated by Palak, I was convinced a little but I had to do something more so that she not only noticed me but also understood my feeling for her, but I was petty sure that Palak and some of my friends from girls side would help me a lot, but I couldn't make myself sit idol and wait for them to do everything for me.

I was dieing to talk to her a single time as I hadn't talked to her yet. I stole every glimpse to see my princess talking, laughing and it seemed heavenly to me.

More than a month passed and all I had done is to see her without knowing her feeling, without knowing her desire, only seeing- seeing and seeing. I wondered some of the time that, she noticed me a hundred times but never objected me, was it a positive response or she just tried to ignores me?

My friend from girl's side told me that she asked them my name. "Asked the name? Why?" Then she told that I always used to stare at her, whenever she saw me, I kept staring at her. They all told her to understand what was going in my mind, and then she smiled. My friend further told me that they had given her a short bio-data of mine.

Now nothing to worry about my bio-data because I know it very clearly that no one from girls could give a wrong detail about me if atleast not polished. I further asked her what my chance to be with her was. She told me, "You are a perfect guy for that girl but she is not of your type". I asked them that what were telling and why were saying so. She clarified me that I always proved to be helpful but she was a little proudy, I always talked with my open heart but she hesitated to talk with.

I then told her that she was a new girl and she might take some time to be frank and I love the girl who is not so much frank with others and every one should be a little proudy so that every one must know his/her status.

I love her charming nature, I love when people talk about her, I love the way she was, I love to watch her, I love each and every attitude of her. The only thing which made me sad was my unfortunate fate, was my luck which was keeping me away from her. I didn't grasp any opportunity to have a chat with her. My greatest problem was then sorted out by Palak when she suggested me that few days later was my birthday and I would have every chance on that day to approach her and no one would feel awkward then at that day.

My heart was dancing recklessly hearing that and from that very moment I was waiting for that great day to arrive.

It was the day of my birthday and as expected I was wished by almost all of my classmates. Birthday wishes were meant not to wish a person but to have a treat to every one who wished the birthday boy and I very frequently use it to get treat and now it was my turn to pay to the rest of the class.

In my school canteen most famous dish for eating was the 'Samosas' and every one loved to eat those. Fortunately or unfortunately I had to give it to every single people of my class. I gave that to everyone and then took one with me for my so called love. It was the only thing by which I could speak to her. I reached nearby her and offered her that samosa.

"No, I cant take it." CUTIE responded denying to grab my offer.

"Please, its my birthday." I was almost begging her to take that.

"I gave it to everyone and they accepted. You can ask your friend, truly it's my birthday." I further said.

"No, I can't accept it from anyone." She finally answered.

After replying she went away. Her negligence was like the explosion of the atom bomb just near to my ear. I could hardly believe her speech. I never thought that any girl could ever reject my offer and especially her rejection was totally beyond the limit of my tube-light, it was truly unexpected.

But I found something special in her rejection which made me happy. As she was the only one who tried to ignore me, made me feel that she was special and need some special treatment. Such sorts of girls who are not influenced by you quickly or make someone feel so, are really good to be influenced or to be loved.

I was not depressed by her ignorance but was much happy as I had grabbed a second for talking with her, though it was too short conversation but it made me glad and I was on the ninth cloud. I knew a second of conversation could be stretched to some minute and then to some hours, I was very hopeful right from the childhood and relied on the latest advertisement which said "baat karne se hi baat banti hai".

That day was good but the next one to be followed would really gonna be bad for me as I had to be away from the school for atleast twenty days on the occasion of marriage ceremony of my cousin brother.

I couldn't understand why people went to such place some ten days before or so and after marriage too they opted to stay there for a week, quite disgusting, I mean what made them glad to do so. Don't they know that they are going to be a burden for the bride's or the groom's family.

Unfortunately my family too was going to stay to the same place for long. It is the ritual here, that close ones should be there atleast a week before marriage. What the people think about themselves? Is it so, that if they are don't going before to their and stay there for long then they are not going to be treated as close ones or will they be neglected by the ceremonial family?

People have there various valid reason for doing so but my personal reason for not going too early was not anyone from my elder who quoted but because of the fact that I didn't want to remain so far from my CUTIE for so long. But if you are not too much grown up or your family didn't think you as a grown up then you have to obey your elders and specially your mom just like a good boy and I had to do the same due to lack of any authentic reason behind not going.

I wanted something bad to happen to me, I wanted high fever to occur or some fracture to any of my bones. It would be little painful but I would love to bear that apart from going too early.

I was very sad at home. I never wanted to be away from my CUTIE so early. I was dreaming with my opened eyes. 'Today she talked to me, may be tomorrow I get a chance to talk again', but all in vain, I was not going school the next day for sure.

I couldn't resist my mom from going. I was crying deep inside but its volume is on mute mode, no one could listen or understand except me and my God. I prayed God to do something and provide me a narrow escape but the almighty didn't bother to listen to little poor boy. I couldn't sleep the whole night thinking about her. I was waiting for the God to do some miracle for me.

The next morning came too early. The time has come to leave the house for twenty odd days, driver was waiting for us. The entire luggage was taken by the driver in the car. As I stepped further my heart was getting heavier and heavier and I was crying continuously though not letting anyone to understand but mom is mom, you can't hide anything from her eyes.

She came closer to me and asked for the reason to cry. I started weeping too much and too loud, seeing this, my mom also started crying and asked me not to weep and to tell the reason. But how could I tell the true reason to her. Anyhow I stopped crying and told my mom that I didn't wish to go too early as I would miss my friend more than anyone else.

Truth was a little different; I could hardly miss my friend but will miss my CUTIE a lot. I was crying for her but how could I tell that to mom. My mom hugged me with all motherly love she had for me and convinced me with love to go with her. I took more than half an hour from my starting scene of crying till the ending. Then too I was kept sobbing. We got in the car but my soul remained in the house.

I was very much like a parrot that time that gets caught up in the cage against his wish and was carried away by someone. We reached our destination and ate the lunch.

Each day there passed like a huge mountain. I made a calendar myself there from the day of my arrival to the day of my departure and cut a day from calendar daily which always made me realize how much more to stay there. Slowly and steadily the marriage day arrived.

People get married to stay together all life but due to this marriage I was separated from my beloved for many days.

I wanted that whole ceremony to end quickly and my due date to departure to arrive shortly. I wanted to see my CUTIE. It has been more than a half month I was restricted from seeing her.

I was waiting very impatiently to see her again. Anything for her glimpse! Till that time, I called a number of times to my friend and asked about her.

'Does she miss my presence? Did she also want me to be there as soon as possible? Does her eyes are always in search of me? Does she miss my habit of staring at her? Does she miss my hesitation of staring at her when our eyes get contacted?' These all were the question going through my mind all the time and I always used to ask those to my friends.

I don't know that, all my habit developed only due to her, made any remark on her heart and mind or not. I wanted her to be mine, forever and ever.

Now the day arrived for us to go back to our home, I was the only who was excited more than anyone. I was too happy for this day. I could see my friends back and more importantly I could see her. I hurriedly picked up my luggage and placed it on the car. My happiness of going home could be seen by anybody and my mother was also not untouched by my move as I often used to ask her the question that when would we go home?

After wishing good bye we went on to our destination. On the way I asked the mom how great it was to go home after such a long time and she replied, "Yes, it was really long time away from home but now we will be there very soon".

We reached home about three hours later. After placing the entire luggage I called my friend to inform him that I was back home and asked him to come home in the evening. My mom went to take a power nap after doing all the house hold chores and getting the house back to the place in the heaven by cleaning every inch of the place.

I felt a little tired but my urge to sleep was miles away from my eyes. How could I have a nap when I was so close to my CUTIE, I had been waiting for this day to arrive from a long time and when it came I was very excited!! I was lost in her thought.

Call- bell rang; I rushed to the door to see who was there at that time in the noon. I was surprised to see Sahil there at that time.

"Hey! What a surprise to see you here!! I was thinking that you would come in the evening."

"What? In the evening? Then what is the time now?" He replied with much amazement.

"Might be 2:30." I told.

"Are you drunk! It's already 5:48." He answered seeing his mobile.

I went to see the time in the clock, another clock, watch, mobile everything which we had, to prove Sahil wrong but nothing happens, all of them showed the timing what Sahil told. How much I was lost in her thought I also don't know. I kept thinking and the time flew away too fast.

We entered my room and started gossiping of here and there. After revolving him round and round in my question related to school and friend I suddenly jumped to ask about her. He laughed as soon as I asked about her. I asked him the reason and he replied, "I was petty sure about it that you would ask about her not at once but sooner".

I asked him to avoid the suspense and to tell everything related to her which he got to know in these days. He told me that she was really nice and honest and trustworthy girl to be hanged on with. I asked him that what did he mean by his words, and was he trying to reflect her quality or giving me the consent to go on her? He said that he meant both. Whatever be his wish I don't care, the thing which I only cared was that he appreciated her and that meant a lot to me, it meant that she was deserveable.

After all, in India people trust more than on their friend for their own love. If someone falls in love and if there friend appreciate the one for whom he/she fell for, then it would be easy for both of them to go further. The appreciation from friend was believed to be the right choice for them whom they hardly ever get in their life.

But my story was a little different; I loved the girl that's why they noticed her and reached to the conclusion to give her a clean chit and me a green signal.

My mom entered the room and Sahil stood up to say 'hello' to my mom. She was pleased to see my friend. She didn't want to interrupt us so she went inside and assured us with nice snacks to be followed soon. We kept talking about here and there, our treasure of talking was not going to be empty so soon, after all we met after such a long time.

Hardly five minutes went, and mother was ready with tray in her hands having a variety of snacks for both of us. Everytime when snacks are presented before Sahil he didn't forget to say, "yaar iski kya zaroorat thi, per leker aa gaye ho to mana to kar nahi sakte hai. Laao-Laao jaldi do bhi ab." Listening to these words I could only smile and my mom was also very much aware with his dialogue.

This time was also none other than any of the previous one, as soon as mom went inside to have some water he uttered his dialogue again. While eating he told me "yaar I almost come to your house daily but your mom never allowed me to go back without having snacks". I took it my turn to crack a joke on him. I said, "My mom knew it very well that you come here only to have it and that's why everytime you come in the evening at the time of refreshment". We suddenly started laughing and now it was time for us to go out.

After eating and drinking I called mom to inform her that we were going out together. She gave the permission to go but asked to come soon. We went out to the local market to have a look. In the market we decided to go to Rajveer's house. We kept walking towards his home, his house was at a little distance of nearly a kilometer from market so we went on foot.

Sahil rang the bell. A while after Rajveer was there to open the gate. We all got inside after a warm hug. As soon as we opened the mouth to abuse him for not calling me he told us in a low pitched voice to be calm and not to abuse here as his father was at home. We wished him. Our image was of a very bright, intelligent, disciplined and a queer boy before him and we didn't want to spoil it in front of him so we kept quite.

Sooner we reached the terrace of his house and then the bad time for Rajveer began, we both started beating and abusing him and only he could do was to say sorry a hundred times. Actually this is the way how a boy meets his close friend after some time. He was lying on the floor and above him was we the Champ as if it was a hard fight of WWE. We stood up finally after the sequel of WWE.

Rajveer said to us, "My father wants me to be as you both are without knowing the fact how idiot, asshole, dumbo you are".

It was more than half an hour being there so we decided to go then, so we went down stairs. Rajveer accompanied us to the main road, there we talked a little standing at the road then Rajveer told us to have cold drink.

We reached the shop to have it. After consuming a sip of drink Sahil alarmed, "O teri this is already expired". We quickly started to find the expiry date but apart from his drink none other was expired. He asked Rajveer to buy a new one for him but he denied. We both know he was not going to divorce the drink he had, even if we gave him the new one. Rajveer clearly declared that he would not spend further a single penny on him; he could either drink or leave it. We were taking sip after a sip and he was bound to see our faces laughing.

He decided to go with the drink he had and took a sip and then, "it is expired. What to do?" Another sip and then, "I don't want to drink but if I leave it then its going to be a waste". Another sip and, "it may harm me but leaving it means loss of money and drink". Another sip and, "friend tell I should leave it or not?" Another sip and it was over. Finally he exclaimed with joy, "paisa wasool". He started taunting Rajveer.

Haramkhor! hans raha hai, agar kuch ho jata to? Sahil.

To saale pine ko kisne bola tha, chor deta. Rajveer.

Saale chor dete to tere baap aate pilane ko. Sahil.

Saale mere baap tere dadaji lagenge, Izzat se naam le apne dadaji ka. Rajveer.

I was standing aside watching them and laughing thoroughly and not only I, they two along with the shopkeeper was also laughing.

I interrupted in between their award winning speech and reminded them that we were getting late, then only they got back to normal. We bid good bye to Rajveer with the hope to meet him tomorrow in the school.

This day was the big day for me. I could see my queen, CUTIE, my everything!! Upto now she meant more than anything to me. If someone would have asked me to stay at home that day then I would surely have passed out. I can die happily after have a glimpse of her. Today was the day I could see her, I had waited a lot for this day to arrive but why too late? It should be much earlier. Nevertheless it lastly arrived. The whole night I didn't sleep. I was very excited and hoping for the night to wind up soon.

I got up early and did all the hanky-panky things and then after dressing up myself for school. I reached the school very early, a very few classmates were present. We all wished each other and a shake of hand followed. They all said that they missed me, they missed my naughtiness, they also asked me about the marriage that how did it go through. I told them it was good although I didn't want to tell it good but I had to.

I was talking to them but my eyes were in search for someone else. Slowly and steadily as time was running everyone was entering the class but not a single sign of her to see her arriving.

I went near the school's main gate so that if she was coming then I could see her from far distance, but then too everyone was entering the gate except her, I couldn't even get her there. I could see all my friends coming. Whenever any girl of my class entered the school, seeing me she passed a smile showing that they were pleased to see me after a long time.

Rajveer, Aakash and all others came, Sahil was yet to come but I was not bothered for him. I had a talk with the friend and asked Rajveer, "Is Tamannah a regular comer or not?" and he assured me about her regularity. We all then see Sahil coming; He directly came to us without going to class to keep his bag. We hugged each other and then Rajveer told him my eagerness to see someone and he understood about whom he was talking.

Sahil told me not to worry for her as he had seen her in school uniform at her gate ready to initiate for school. I and Sahil both come through the same way. I was much relieved by his words. But till now I didn't know her house, Sahil did know and we both followed the same path that rode to her house. He often tried to make me recognize her house in the class whenever I asked for but everytime I failed.

It was hardly two minutes for the bell to ring but she was nowhere. I was eagerly waiting for her and was getting drowned in the deep ocean of mind just to wait for her.

It was just some second before the bell to ring that I saw someone very similar to her in every aspect coming from the same path, my queen used to take for school. Her body structure, her face, her walking style, everything was not an inch different from my CUTIE. She was yet at a long way from school and I was seeing her standing nearby the gate. In one go I was thinking her to be my CUTIE but one thing which made her apart from CUTIE was that she was wearing the school shirt and skirt which almost everyone wore in the school. I didn't identify her, as my CUTIE used to wear the suit.

As she came closer her face could be seen with much clarity, and seeing her I jumped in the air, my friend made a tight grip on me so that I could not repeat it again, atleast not near the gate and office. They all knew that I had seen her and so it was the reflection of my happiness after seeing her.

At that time my friends were teaching me the lesson how to behave in school, how to act in such situation. They were pretending to be some sadhoos or parents having good oratory skill, and at the same time they were dragging me to the ground near the gate itself.

saala pagal ho gaya hai usko dekh kar. Sahil.

Door rakh-door rakh saale ko tamannah se. Sirf dekh kar ye haal hai agar proposal accept ki tab to kamina khushi se mar jayega. Rajveer.

They were forcing me against my wish. Now the bell rang and it was the time for all to gather in line according to class in the ground. She also came and I started repeating my habit of staring at her.

I asked Rajveer, "when she started wearing skirt?"

He replied, "soon after you went".

I love to see her in any dress but I like her more in her earlier avatar. Anyway it doesn't matter what she wears, what matter is that I love her and she is right in front of me. I can see her; I am seeing her and will always see her.

My attention was not on the prayer, not on what the principal's advice and speech but only on her. Assembly was over and we all reached the class. I was on my bench and she was just opposite to me in opposite row. I kept staring at her and it was hard for her to look back at me. While I was seeing her in class all the girls were giggling at me. I looked back at them but then too they continued. They might be thinking me as a dog which stuck back to its habit and the dog like me had the habit of staring CUTIE.

I was seeing her after a long time and wanted to continue without any disturbance but how could this happen in a place totally filled with your friends. Whenever I got the chance I looked at her no matter who was there in the class.

At lunch time some girls talked to me about my wellbeing and exclaimed that they felt good to see me there. They said they missed me but missed my staring more than me; they missed my naughtiness, and my presence.

Palak said that she kept a close watch on me today as she knew me very well that I would not let any chance away for looking at her and further told me to have patience as I was fully on as soon as I entered the class.

From now on I decided to have some patience atleast for today but things were not so easy for me. I was told by Sahil that the monthly tests would be held soon. He further told me to avoid her for some time and focus on my studies as the math's teacher was very strict and hardly allowed someone to pass in his paper. I was little nervous as I didn't know the syllabus and haven't yet started. He also told that our civics and economics teacher were also too miser in giving the numbers.

Our math's teacher was though very open by his heart, but too strict in awarding numbers. His name was 'Rajnikant' and his habit was to come ten minutes late into the class as per the scheduled time of the subject and ten minutes of teaching and after that gossiping for some time and then departed ten minutes before the time. He was too fast in class. Understanding math in class and ofcourse from him was bit too hard.

And same was the situation of our civics and economics teacher. He often came on time but never tried to make us understand the topic. He relied more on reading than anything else that is why he started reading the every single words in book. As soon as he entered the class he picked the book of any student and a boring reading got started. After reading the topic completely he made someone stand among and asked to read the same topic again and after that someone else would continue it. He was such a yuck. We had never seen him smiling.

Sahil's advice was in favor of me but to ignore her was just similar to be away from oxygen though knowing that it will take away the life of any living being in a few minutes only. I knew I had to work hard for the test to attain good marks but I decided not to keep her aside rather, to take her and studies hand in hand. It was difficult to do so but I was determined to take that risk for her and if, her thought gonna affect my study then I had to look for some alternative way.

Now I was much more cautious about her and the studies. In the school I stole each single glimpse of her which I could, and if I had to summarize the day then I could only tell that it was a great and perfect day for me as my CUTIE was there infront of my eyes the whole day.

After dismissal I went to the coaching which was run by our school teacher named 'Vilas Rao', I was the most intelligent, sincere, honest, disciplined, hard working, soft boy in the school according to him. He cared for me and I too respected him and appreciated his knowledge.

I used to go to his coaching where a number of students from each class came to gain knowledge. He was very familiar with my family as he occasionally used to come to my place to meet my family and always gave an excellent feedback of mine, he not only told so but also he really meant what he said. He was well educated and had a vast teaching experience of not less than twenty-five years, so he knew what I was going to do in the future.

Having classes from him not only cleared my basics but also helped me attain good marks in all exam, apart from it I have learnt a lot more from him. He was not only a good teacher for me but also he was my guide who always tried to push me ahead by appreciating me, increasing my moral as if he was my family member.

I reached home in the evening and from thereon I started to think about my love or my one sided love for her. I thought about her but everytime my thought got stuck to her uniform. She now wears everything apart from suit which made me to think about it again and again.

When I first saw her she was in her suit in which she resembled like as suit is only made for her! But 'what happened to her now? Why did she wear skirt? Is she too having complexion for suit as a few of such can be counted?' I thought for it more than her but couldn't reach any conclusion for my queries. Anyway not to bother so much for her dress but only for her!!

I got to know from some one of my friend that she too enjoyed my staring nature, which I thought to be a good sign and a slight green signal from her side. I had a number of questions in my mind and its answers could only be given by her.

'Does she like me? Does she love me? Did she ever accept my love? Did she like or want to have my company? Did she too have the same feeling for me? Does she understand the reason behind seeing her everytime?'

All such type of question was running in my mind with a very high priority in my life. Questions were in abundance but the answers for them were unknown. I went to prepare myself after coming out from her dream for the test that was scheduled next week. Time was too little for me to prepare, anyhow I was studying honestly to have upper hand in class and to gain good marks.

I went through the books of NCERT thoroughly, and sometimes preferred some reference books too, but I knew that in this limited time, only NCERT books can be proved to be helpful so I gave much preference to it.

Now the time arrived for the monthly tests. We all had to sit in the exam according to our roll number. I prepared for the test very well and in the morning we all friends discussed the topic from the subject whose test was going to be held today. We wished good luck to friends and got into the class and acquired our seat.

On due time test was over and it was good as far as my context. Tests lasted for a week and in between tests we had our usual classes. All the paper of mine was good.

Classes were going on in the school, all came to school to study but I went there just to see her and getting lost in her. I didn't do anything except for looking at her. I asked Palak to do something for me or else my life would be a hell, it was very difficult to bear the pain to see her in class but not getting any chance to talk.

She too might be aware of my feeling as till now everyone knew that I love her then how was it possible that my feeling was untouched by her and if she was aware then what the hell was she waiting for? Why didn't she give me any sign either positive or negative or if not that then she should have atleast told that to someone and I was sure the person whom she would tell would surely come and clarify everything from her aspect.

One thing was sure that whatever would be her decision for me I was neither going to leave her nor was I going to make her uncomfortable with any sort of cheap activities. If she rejected me then too she would be in my heart forever and ever and I was truly not going to hang on with any other girl in my whole life. It was my true love for her and true love is not mend to happen again and again, it happens a single time with a really special one like her. Even if she denied my proposal then I would love to die keeping her in my heart for ever rather than to go for any other girl.

She was not showing any signs of likes or dislikes. 'Is she trying to ignore me? Isn't she taking me seriously? Did she want me to continue a little more of my habit before declaring something? Did she too want me to look at her? God knows better what she is thinking and what I have to do'.

A day in the school Sahil came and told me that he was passionate about 'her'. I asked him for whom was he telling.

He replied, "I am telling it for Ruksar".

I told him to go and have a talk to her. I was the person telling him to directly go and talk even knowing that it is more than two months and I haven't yet spoken a word to CUTIE apart from the one on my birthday. Sahil told me that it was not going to be beneficial enough, firstly he had to make her realize that he liked her. I asked him how? O'er that he asked me to let it do it on his own.

I just said to him and warned him, "I tell you better need someone from her friend to let her realize or else you will be hanging like a pendulum moving here and there and not having any fixed or stable position".

Rajveer took the turn to depress him. He suggested him to try something smartly or she was very frank and open and could easily be fled away from him with someone. Sahil was not depressed by our speech and said to us "Sali jaye to jaye, ek jayegi to dusri aayegi. Konsa hume shadi karni hai usse". He asked me to have a bet.

"What type of bet?" I asked.

Then he disclosed that the bet was for us, and asked me to let us see that who had her girl first, who would make his girlfriend first. It was just for fun and may be due to this we accelerated our job. I found it a little funnier but though entertaining. I accepted it and from then we were more attentive towards our girl.

Next day I went to school after planning from home how to win that bet and for the same cause I thought to involve my best friend from girls side or the girl I liked the most among the girls apart from my CUTIE, my CUTIE was always on the top and all the top hundred ranks were acquired by her alone in my priority list.

Her name was Shalini D'souza. She was a good girl, very frank and helpful and talkative. She talked too quickly and I liked her conversation in English the most. Actually she was from Kerala so her English was fluent and attractive. She was very helpful towards me.

When I reached school I met her as usual and said to her that I had to tell her something and then she was more eager than a small kid to know it quickly. I told her that I liked someone and she was too smart to understand about whom I was taking about. I thought that it was not her smartness but mine which made her understood even before telling the name. Its not good to take the credit as their was not a single student in the class who didn't know about it. Anyway she asked me to continue and I orated the whole scenario to her. She kept smiling from the time I started to tell her my feeling, but she assured to help me in such situation as I was expecting the same from her.

I didn't know that what she would do but her assurance made me feel much relived. She was the one to be trusted.

I was a very famous boy in the class and especially among girls then too how didn't she notice me yet or she had but was she a too much shy to accept it openly. Every girl from my class except for few, were busy in clearing the path for me. I haven't told anyone except Shalini to do some favor but the consequence was different and all were busy talking with

Tamannah and they always created a scenario to start telling her about me everytime.

Why were all the girls doing so? I didn't have any idea!! May be it was my well beingness towards them from childhood due to which they were helping me at the time of need without even asking me to do so. I didn't know about the above situation if those girls hadn't told me.

Each day they talked to her and at the lunch time or any leisure. They all came into the class, surrounded me, and told me about what they did that day, what they talked and how was the response. They also told me that she was showing some interest in me as they started telling her about me. They also told me that sometimes they pinched her by calling out my name along with her and she simply smiled at them.

If I was getting surprised by the work of the girls then what would have she thought of them and me. She might have thought what type of boy was I, as all the girls were always appreciating me and the question that would prick her would be that why did these girls do so? Were they been told to do so? She also might be intended to know the reason for girls behavior towards her.

I took my study and her smoothly and simultaneously. When I was away from her dream I used to study with my mind and heart open and after studying I was again back to her thought. When I had to study again I said sorry to her dream to leave her in between and then went to study further. When at home I preferred myself to be alone than to be surrounded by people so that I could easily get into her dream and fantasy.

Day by day we submitted our progress report in the field of love and we dealt in percentage and that percentage was awarded by our judges; Rajveer and Aakash. I and Sahil told everything about the day and they then replied us with the percentage of progress we had. Till then my progress was only

2% and that of Sahil was 1%. I was happy to be ahead of him but the margin was too less.

Till then when I used to see her she turned her face other side but while turning her face she usually smiled so lightly so that no one could understand, and now our eyes got contacted more often than before, which I considered to be a good move, thinking, the hard work of all the girls and Shalini was getting reflected in little packets.

I wanted something more than that. I wanted to talk to her but anyway something was better than nothing. I got to know about her all from Shalini and many of the girls.

Whenever teacher asked her any question or told her to stand then all the boys of class started chanting my name as if the teacher told me to stand or to answer. If she was unable to answer the question then the boys and girls both pinched me from behind and when I looked back then they simply said to tell her the answer. I could only smile at them and their naughtiness and somewhere in my heart I loved to be taunted and was happy that people add her name with mine.

Upto now if there was a girl from the fifth standard then she would have surely known everything going on within me for her and know what is going on in my mind but which type of clay did God use to create her is known to Him only, no sign, no emotion, nothing. May be she wanted to check and conform my behavior as a boy but not as a classmate.

"I have something to tell you." Palak said.

"What? Tell me?" I asked her with curiosity.

"Yesterday I talked to her and asked her whom she thought to be a good boy in the class." Palak.

"What she told?" I asked her with an increasing curiosity.

"She told that she hates boys." Palak replied.

"What?" I was shocked to know her unexpected reply.

"Yes." Palak.

"But why?" I was still shocked.

"She didn't reply to this." Palak.

"It means I don't have any chance to be with her, she is not going to be mine." I was depressed.

"It doesn't mean you lost the chance. Everyone need a man to live her life and you are the one perfect enough for every girl and if ever she didn't accept your proposal then it means she really didn't deserve you. Don't lose your heart and try to talk with her if not directly then indirectly making someone a mediator. I am damn sure and can have a bet that she will accept you and your love. Why to worry, all the girls are with you and you have some very good friends too." Palak tried to handle the situation.

'I know she was right but it hurt me and I was very desperate to have her in my life. Without having a word of love with her she became my life. I could never think of living without her and then her statement that she hated the boys really hurt me. I felt as if my heart was getting pinched with the nail again and again. My mind stopped thinking but somewhere inside I had a strong hope that she will surely love me someday. I truly had a innocent love for her. I didn't want anything in return except my CUTIE. I love her from deep inside and how it could be possible to forget about her only by a simple sentence she uttered. May be she didn't like the boys because of roughness, arrogance, their mentality and cheap activity which they usually perform. May be possible that when she knows me better, her thinking would change and think that I am not such type of boy and may be possible that she also have a strong desire for me.' I said to myself and tried to make me understand and allowed a ray of hope to enter in me.

The copy of monthly tests were checked and the parents-teachers meeting was to be held on the coming Saturday. My all papers went good so I didn't have the fear to be scolded at home but a great fear or you may call it to be a routine which should be followed at every meeting. I now feared less as I was getting used to with it since childhood and now my mother too scolded me less in school thinking me as a grown up. We were not interested in seeing our copy rather much more interested in seeing others copy and this was the habit of everyone.

If someone got less marks in any subject then he didn't recall the reason but started searching some other whose condition was same as him so that they may create a group of having less marks, if ever someone asked the reason of getting less marks then apart from giving reason they would tell that they were not alone but a number of student were there having less marks. Teachers were blamed for that thinking that they didn't check the copy properly otherwise not so much people would get such bad marks.

The days passed and now it was Saturday, the day for the meeting in the school. My mom was always ready for such day to come and to get my feedback and also to see my progress in result. It was 10 o' clock and my mother asked me to get ready to go as she had already started to make herself presentable. My mom had not forgotten such day in my school life upto today a single time. Sometimes when I didn't want to go out of fear of having not much good mark in paper or when I forgot about the day then my mom reminded me of going.

I got myself ready for the school and mom kept reminding me to be quick. Anyhow we reached school and went to our respective classes where answer sheets of our tests were shown. My class teacher 'Miss Nita' was sitting with the answer sheet of all the students of our class. We went in; I wished her and my mom sat on the chair in front of my class teacher when offered. She appreciated my mom for being a regular visitor for such meeting.

She gave mom my answer sheets to have a look on what had I done, my mom saw them very closely and keenly and then after satisfying with the marks she signed on the slot provided for the parents. Then after mom handed back the paper to Miss Nita, she then started querying about me and my behavior, Miss Nita looked at me and at that time I went right back of my mom and signaled my teacher not to give any bad feedback. She smiled a little and then replied my mom with a positive feedback only.

I was happy to hear that but my mom was surprised to hear that as she always listened as "Your ward is very sincere and disciplined to teacher and also very bright in study but too naughty for their class mate. He teases others and gives the nick name to everyone, always wants to dominate the class. Many are afraid of him".

Today my mom was getting a good response about me, but I knew it wouldn't be digestive for her. We went back for home, not knowing about mom but I was very happy for the reason that today I was not going to be scolded either for the marks or for my feedback.

In the middle of our way to home my father called to know my result and mom told him everything happened in school. She told him that my marks were good and something which was unpredictable happened. When father asked her about that unpredictable thing, she replied the teacher's response for me, her feedback which I didn't get in the entire previous years. After a while he disconnected the call.

We reached home till then and I felt much relaxed that day. As soon as I entered my room I lost in my CUTIE's dream and don't know when I fell to sleep.

Sahil came in the evening to meet me and we went upstairs to the top floor. We talked there sometimes and then we saw my mom present before us having a tray in her hand filled with snacks. When mom went down, he didn't forget to push forward his famous dialogue for the snacks.

We ate them and discussed about the exam. We discussed on our latest burning topic and asked for the idea to impress her or some valid reason to talk to her. I also told him what Palak told me and was a boy not to bother about anything.

He lived happily and wanted me to be the same, he told me not to panic but to try hard continuously for her and the day would surely come when she would me mine only. He better knew how much I loved her and couldn't even think to live without her.

Everyone in the class knew about me and my true love for her and that was the reason why people appreciated me and tried to do something better what they could do for me to make me and her together. One thing I needed to tell that I didn't tell anyone to do a favor for me except for the Shalini, I only sometimes asked them some queries about her and they all did the favor by their will without my wish, as I only wished for Shalini to help me.

Days are passing by and in a week it is going to be the summer holidays which would not be less than one and half month and this was going to be a tension for me as I didn't even have a talk with her in the approximately 3 months.

In the school I was little down and many asked me the reason for that but I kept silent. I told Rajveer and Sahil the reason and they asked me to go and directly talk to her and do friendship with her.

'If I could do this when why the hell I waited for three months but who will make them understand'.

I didn't have any past experience in this subject, and in his field experience is counted. I was a new comer in this field so little terrified and didn't know what to do. I was terrified just like a kid going to attend the school first time; he doesn't know what will happen to him there. That day I asked Sahil to let me see her house at dismissal and he agreed.

I was waiting for the dismissal impatiently and at the schedule time the bell rang. I gave my bag to a junior studying in the same coaching to take my bag away. I went with Sahil to have a look to her house. We were going through the same path which we took for to school and home. After two minutes of walk Sahil put up his finger towards a house and said "It is the house of Tamannah".

I was, a little shocked to see that house it was on the right side of the lane and I used to take that way from my childhood and from then onwards I knew that house, but never thought it to be Tamannah's house. I asked Sahil again if he was sure for it and he replied, "Yes, I am sure. I have seen her many times coming out from it to go school and also at the time of returning from school she went to the same house".

Her house was just on my way to school and home and good enough for me to look while with a sight while going school. Seeing her house I started singing the song on which Sahil too accompanied me and the song was,

`Ghar se nikalte hi, kuch door chalte hi, raste me hai uska ghar.`

Since then everyday when I got out for school I was in the hope to see her early at her home on the way. May be I get a glimpse of her. When I was about to cross her house I slowed down my bicycle to increase the response time but I couldn't find her anywhere. I went through the same way from my childhood but I never saw her, it was more than eight years but never saw her a single time and if that was her house then she truly belonged from a good family. A family having self respect and know how to keep their children not exposed.

I haven't seen her in those eight odd years which meant that they knew the meaning of house; they knew how to be in a society. I often saw everyone from nearby her house and someone opposite to her house sitting on the lane and talking but never saw her or anyone from her house doing so.

Time was getting close for the school to close for summer vacation. That day in school, things were normal, normal for me to stare her, normal for her to not give any signal or sign, normal for me to stare her continuously and again normal for her to ignore that and smile in her heart.

At the time of lunch Shalini came to me happily and said that she had something good news for me. I knew something good happened as she was much excited that time.

"Tell me what you have for me?" I enquired.

"Today I told her about you and about your famous habit and asked her how she thinks when she encounter you seeing, then she told that "whenever he sees me I don't know what to do, I feel shy and so I am not able to look at that side out of shyness and make my head lying down and that is the only reason why I don't sit in front side but internally I feel very much shy and I don't know what happened to you all, everytime you all are talking to me but not talking about me but talking about him only"". Shalini explained the exact wordings of my CUTIE.

"Oh! Whenever she shifts her head other side I thought she tried to ignore me but now I could understand she did it due to her shyness." I felt good to know and was relaxed.

"I also asked her that whether she knew you love her?" Shalini said.

"What she replied then?" My eagerness was on the top.

"Too eager to know that!!!" Shalini tried to tease me.

"Please don't create much suspense, tell it quickly." I begged her to speak the reality.

"She told she knew that." Shalini said smiling at me.

"Then did you ask her whether she too liked me or not?" I questioned her.

"Yes, I did ask." Shalini.

"What she answered then?" I asked again.

"She said that she doesn't know whether she liked you or not but also tells that she likes your habit to stare at her without thinking who is in the class and always take risk to see her when class is being taken by the most furious teacher of school 'Mr. Joseph'." Shalini said.

Shalini further told me to continue my hard work, "today she liked your habit and tomorrow she will surely like you. And by the way I am with you and not only I, but also all the class is with you. All want you two to be together. We will make her change her mind for you. We all will do it together along with your hard work."

"Why do you always stare her? What do you feel in doing so?" Shalini questioned.

"Whenever I see her I feel relaxed and want to fell so continually so I did it regularly." I answered her.

"Thank God she is the one whom you stare at otherwise if someone else was in her place then your habit would have fired her." Shalini said.

"One thing more, if she didn't tell it or got fed up with your habit or didn't tell it in wrong way to anyone then it means she is absolutely having a soft corner for you. You will have her someday very soon." Shalini added just virtually congratulating me for my good progress.

I was damn happy to hear what she said and I started seeing dream of her with my eyes wide opened. I told everything what Shalini told me to my friends and they too were happy for me.

Sahil was also busy these days with his girl and tried everything to be noticed by her whether he was in class or outside the class and more often he was being noticed. We told our progress to our judge with pride and they declared the result.

Today I had got 10% marks which meant I had to continue my hard-work to convert that ten percent into hundred. My work of last three months made me achieve that percentage. I knew it was too slow but slowly and steadily I would reach the peak.

We were getting holiday homework by our subject teacher and the vacation was just a few days to start, all were telling there friend where to go this holiday and asked about the others plans to rejoice. All were a little depressed to be away for such a long time but we had the backup as we all had to attend our coaching classes and it was not going to remain close so we would be in contact with our friends.

Though its true that we will be in contact but the pleasure of doing mischief in class was a far too interesting, whatever we could do outside can never displace the entertainment done in class by a single inch. I was too much worried for the holidays. Holiday this time meant no school, no entertainment, no CUTIE, no staring, no shyness, no teasing by her name, no nsp for seeing her, no cute smile, no eye contact nothing.

My life was going to be in a mess for a long time. How could I live without seeing her? I would be away from my CUTIE for too long, this made me extreme sad. Last few days in school passed as there was nothing left for me. I was sad by my heart and everyone knew that, but nothing could be done at that moment.

Now I started seeing her much more often than before as I knew school would be closed too soon, so I wanted to see her as much as I could and wanted to store her image in my heart which could be recalled during the vacation.

It was the last day before vacation. I went to school singing the song and riding the cycle by taking the same path. When

I reached closer to her house I slowed down my bicycle as usual but she was nowhere. Till now I haven't seen her a single time on her gate ready to proceed for school or else otherwise while going to school. But there was always a hope to see her someday, I was very hopeful. I reached school before time and went to class; some of the classmates were already present. We wished each other and shook hand and some usual talk followed. Today everyone was busy with their friend so that they could spend little more time together before the final bell.

I was surrounded by the boys and chit-chat were going on, everyone trying to tease other, everyone trying to make fun of others, all were together having a good time. A friend told us "I am going to spend the vacation with kothe-wali. I will f**k her whole vacation". That boy was an idiot and always did some sort of mischief which couldn't be considered as naughtiness rather cheap.

By the word kotha he meant to say the place where villains and heroes used to go in the older Hindi movies to entertain themselves. We all knew that he was not going for any such places; the purpose was only to reflect him different than others and to make us laugh.

In the class I didn't bother about the teachers but only to look at her. I didn't listen any word of the teacher but kept seeing at her. Teacher too didn't seem in the mood to teach but were gossiping with all of us as it was the last day of school and they too wanted themselves to have much interaction with us today. Their not being in the mood to teach gave me the reason to smile, now I could see her regularly as teacher was busy talking with student.

I continuously kept staring at her without a blink of my eye and she knew that very clearly. Hena told me with activity of hands that when did the black-board shift this way. I smiled and answered her that at the day when CUTIE took admission in that class. I too giggled. Hena was in the mood to do something. She asked me to wait and turn around to talk with Tamannah. She told something in her ear and CUTIE turn around to look at me. I was amazed to see that. I was very happy that she turned at me but didn't know the reason to look at me.

'What did Hena tell her? I don't know but want to know.' CUTIE then turned as she was before, and Hena kept smiling and telling me "are you satisfied now and happy that she turned at you?" I told her "I am happy but never satisfied even if you make her to sit with me for ever, then also I will never stop seeing her".

"What you did is nice for me but what did you tell into her ears?" I questioned her.

"I simply said that you were calling her." Hena replied.

"And she trusted what you said?" I again queried.

"Yes idiot, that's why she turned to you." Hena clarified.

"Ok! Thank you." I showed her gratitude.

"For what?" She asked amazingly.

"For making her turn around, for me." I answered.

"This is only for you. Actually I can't see you struggling hard to have a glimpse of her, so I thought to lessen your pain and the result, you know it better than me." Hena.

These all our conversation was going on by the activities of the hands and sometimes using some symbols.

My friend wanted to interrupt in between but seeing me busy he left his thought. After conversation with Hena I turned around and acquired attention of my entire friends to tell them what happened just now.

Rajveer turned to see CUTIE and then said, "He is telling lie, she is not seeing her". Everyone believed me except Rajveer. He told me to do that again, I tried to make him understand that I didn't call her rather Hena did that for me, but he was a different man. Everytime he needed a proof. He was such an asshole.

Now the final bell for the dismissal rang and I was crying somewhere very deep for being separated from her for so long time. Everyone was busy wishing a very happy holiday, hugging each other, reminding to call frequently. I was also one of them but my mind was searching her. I knew that she would be lost and I couldn't see her for many days, so I just wanted to look at her continually as much as I could.

All were telling each other that they will miss them but I didn't tell that to anyone. I was going to miss my CUTIE only and no one else. We bid good bye to our friends. When I was about to leave for coaching, I looked for her the last time taking deep breathe for sometime standing at the gate of school. She was having fun with friends and also seemed ready to go home.

Anyway I reached coaching but I felt myself lost. I was in the coaching physically, but mentally besides my CUTIE. Now I won't see my CUTIE anymore for a long time.

Every second of my alone time was being spend on her thought. If someone would have seen me in such situation then he would have told me a man of lay. I had a lot of work to do but I wasn't interested in doing any of them. I reserved myself in my room and went out very occasionally or when it was very urgent or when someone called to come. I had lost interest in everything.

I neither study nor did any work. Everytime I thought for her as if I was addicted to her. Yes, I was addicted to her, addicted to her face, addicted to her cute smile, addicted to her shyness, addicted to her vast glowing eyes, addicted to see her everyday, addicted for the jokes which my friend cracked on us, addicted to talk about her. Now there was no one to tease me taking her name, no one to whom I could share my feelings for her. I missed her very badly and also knew that there might be a time in the whole day when she too would be missing me, it didn't matter for how long.

It was very hard for me to pass the days without her. Each day resembled like an year. It looked like as if the time got stuck itself to somewhere. I wanted the time to pass quickly, but it was much slower than a snail. I wished if she also studied in the same coaching then I could get a look of her charm.

I started finding her coaching and told everyone of my friend to look for her and whenever they find it they had to make a call to me. After a few days Rajveer called me to tell that he knew where she went to take tuition. I asked him and he told me to come home in the evening. I called Sahil and asked him to come in the evening. I waited too hard for evening.

Sahil came at the right time, we together went to Rajveer and on the way I give him the reason to go. When we reached there Rajveer opened the door and asked us to come in. We went inside. He took us to his top most floors and pointed towards a building and said,

"Tamannah took the tuition there."

"There? From whom?" I further enquired of the coaching.

He said, "Actually she is not being taught by a professional but who taught her is her relative and her name is 'Ritika kashyap'. I know her and she is my father's student."

I asked the timing and he said to me that it was the same when I reached his home, he also told me to stay there for some times and to go only at the time when she would be returning back to home. We stayed there having funny talks; no one was ready to lose a chance of making fun of others. Rajveer came to us and told to leave now as it was the time for her to leave for home.

We went outside and waited for her on the middle of the road, after sometime we saw her sitting on a rickshaw along with a little boy. Rajveer told me that he was her brother and both were taking the tuition there. Now I knew where she went for the tuition and where I should be if I wanted to see her during holidays.

Since then I used to go to Rajveer's place regularly in the evening exactly the same time as of her tuition to see her. At the time of her returning home I took Rajveer with myself to the road and waited for her to pass by, we waited at such a place, from where, only we could see her and when she made herself turn back then only she could see us. It was our regular routine now to go and stay there just to have a glimpse of her. Sahil too was free in the evening so he also accompanied me to Rajveer's house.

Till then he too got to know about Ruksar's house and insisted us to go with him, there, may be he too got a chance to see her, may be she was on her terrace which let him see her. In love, though, we all know chances are very negligible to see your loved one in such cases and all depend on luck, but on that condition we made ourselves too much hopeful. We rely more on may be like condition.

Though Ruksar's house was a just double of Rajveer's house in term of distances to be covered to reach there but we had to go, after-all he was our friend and he too accompanied me everywhere we asked him. We didn't go there regularly but very rarely being little far away.

When I saw my CUTIE regularly I was getting back to conscious stage from sub-conscious stage. Now I took interest in studying and work also. I started doing the homework given to us for the vacation. In a day I completely did hard job and finished one assignment. Some took two days but anyhow all getting completed in a day or two which meant I would get a lot of free time after the completion of my homework. More time for me means more her thought, more her dream. I became regular visitor of Rajveer home and we all had a good time altogether.

Whenever I had to go somewhere for work, I used to take the path which rode to Tamannah's house, in a hope that might be today I could get to see her which never happened to me. When I didn't have the work on that way then too I covered the distance of her house being known very clearly that the work for which I went out didn't exist anywhere on that way but in the totally different way, and for that I had to cover two kilometers extra to reach there, but I loved to bear that pain than to lose any chance for her.

Holiday was a too long for people like me who couldn't bear to stay further apart anymore. I used to see her regularly without her knowledge for this act. I had to go to my village to enjoy the vacation for sometime, as stated by my father. He wanted me to go there to meet the grandparents and to stay there for a few days so that my grandparents would be pleased to have me and also to enjoy with the fruits like Mango, Litchi and every single seasonal fruit.

We had a plenty of uncountable mango trees there. I did want to meet my grandparents, but I didn't want to stay there for more than two days. But my father insisted me on staying there for atleast ten or more days.

'How to make him understand, that I couldn't stay for so long time, away from my CUTIE. If I went there then how could I see her!!'

I didn't tell anything to father because I knew if I told him then he would take me in his consent to stay there for as much time as he wanted, so I preferred to stay quiet and said to my self "let me reach there first and I will make my grandparents to understand for not being there for much time".

I started packing to leave for the village. My mom bought a lot of things from market for everyone there. A lot of things means, a lot bulky, a lot to carry. I was going there alone and all the luggage would be carried by me only. I asked mom, "why to give me so many things to take away." Then she replied, "You are going to your grandparents home and are you thinking to go there empty handed?" She also made me understand what to give and to whom. I packed everything necessary to start my journey the next day in the morning.

I went up from bed early in the morning. I went to fresh myself. I came out after the bath. Mom was ready with the breakfast in her hand for me. I asked her to keep that on the bed. I was dressing myself to leave, seeing me busy, she took up the plate of breakfast and give it in my mouth taking out a piece from the whole.

This is what only a mother can do. She knows everything about their child and knows what we require at what time and does everything for us at the right time. As I was moving here and there in search of something or to take something, she too did the same for me to have the breakfast with the plate in her hand.

I dressed myself completely and then I asked my mom to go and do something else as I would eat that myself without troubling her. She denied and wanted to continue it as I have to wash my hand before and after then I sat there and she let me eat the whole breakfast by her own sweet hands.

I stood up to leave then but my mom asked me to stay there, I knew what was she is going to do. She was chanting some mantras from the holy Quran and then she would blow the air of her mouth on me, which is called "DUM KARNA" then only she would allow me to go. She never allowed me to go anywhere without doing the same from my childhood.

Whenever she did it then she asked me to leave and reminded me to call her as soon as I reached the destination.

We bid ALLAH HAFIZ to each other then I started my journey. I took the bus directly going to my village. I got in the bus and occupied a seat there. The whole journey I only thought about my CUTIE sitting near the window. I recalled everything related to us and every thing I did in school and her reaction for that. I was lost in her thoughts; I didn't know where the bus reached till then. I turned my face to see outside after a while I recognized the location outside which was the symbol that I had reached my village and soon would be off from bus.

I reached the village. I took a rickshaw from there as I had much luggage to carry on; otherwise I would have gone there on foot. It was hardly two minutes walk from the bus stop to our home. I got seated myself on the rickshaw. On the way I thought it was some five hour drive from the city to my village and I didn't know when it started and when finished. It was her thought only which made it happen. This is the power of love which made you lost anywhere at anytime.

I reached my home. My grandmother was waiting for me, seeing me she came closer and I wished her Salaam, she answered me and hugged me and a kiss on my forehead. She was too happy to see me there after-all I was the eldest grandson. My aunt was also there with uncle and their children, I wished them too and in return I was being wished by their children as all were younger than me. Her youngest son came running to me calling me 'bhaiya' loudly. I threw him in air as he came to me and caught him when he came down. Grandmother asked me to sit beside her, and then a round of question answer session went on.

"How is your mother? Your father? Why didn't they also come along with you? How was your journey? Did you face any hardship? Is everything alright there?" were the some question frequently asked, whenever I went there. While we were talking, my aunt was ready with the lunch, she called out me for the lunch. I asked grandmother for lunch and she also came with us. She said that everyone was waiting for me and no one was ready to eat without me even Fazal, my youngest cousin. I asked them to sit as I had to make a call to my mom.

I called her, she picked up the call, I informed her about my wellness and also that I had reached there safely. After a few more exchange of words I hanged off the phone and went to have lunch as I was feeling hungry and also all were waiting for me to sit there so I had to go, so that they could proceed eating.

We ate the lunch, it was much delicious. I ate as much as I could. I then sat by my grandmother to talk to her. I was surrounded by my all cousin, they sat surrounding me. All were quarreling with each other to have a seat very close to me and we were seeing them with a smile on our face. They loved me a lot and I too loved them very much. I told my eldest cousin among them to pick up my bag there. She went on and came dragging my bag and saying, "bhaiya have you brought any brick or something like that, it's so heavy."

Seeing her struggling all my cousin went to help her and brought the bag to me. I opened the bag and gave the whole packet of chocolate to Fazal which I personally bought for him, everyone's eyes were on that chocolate so I told him to share it among them and he agreed. No one of my own sister or anyone among my cousin ever tried to disobey what I said.

Then one by one I gave everyone what I had for them or what mom gave me for them. They were very happy when I gave them all. Now it was turn for my aunt, I gave her what mom had given for her. Now I turned to grandmother, mom gave her in a packed plastic bag for her and I didn't bother to know what she had given.

Mom's gifts were too much appreciated by my cousins; they quickly called my mom and thanked her for sending them the present. Later on aunt too had a chat with mom and then my grandmother. I told grandmother that I was going out. She signaled me to go. I asked Fazal if he wished to come with me, and he followed me happily.

I went out to meet grandfather and uncle. Uncle was not present there but grandfather was. I wished Salaam and he replied. He asked me the time of my arrival to the village and many more such question as like grandmother asked. I stood up to move from there as I knew it was his time to rest and if I would have been there then he won't take rest so I preferred to leave. I took Fazal and went on to the house of my grandmother's brother.

He too was just like grandfather to us. We went there inside to make them surprised, but they all seemed to know everything about me. I heard them talking about me. They were discussing and assuming that whether I reached or not or was I about to reach.

I went infront of them in a room; all were sitting in the same room. I wished everyone there, seeing me standing in front of them they were happy. I sat there and then a never ending talk started. 'Phuphi' or 'Bua' brought some snacks for me as I told them before that I already had the lunch. They all knew that I loved chocolate candies so they asked me to take some snacks if I wanted the candy. They had the candy in their hand so I took up some snacks to get the candy.

I took the snacks for just formality and then I got the whole candies. I always have chocolate candies with myself wherever I go since my childhood and the candy was given to me by my mom only. She gave the whole packet to me before going anywhere; only difference was that, in childhood I used to get a packet of lollypop, but now a packet of 'kaccha mango bite' which I like the most. At home too, my mom brought the candy and gave it to us daily, but not more than two in a day. Whenever I ate a candy or any chocolate I didn't throw the wrapper but I collected them in a packet.

Staying there for an hour I wished then to go home as suddenly something ran into my mind and made me remember about some stuffs. I had forgotten to bring something for grandmother, what mother had given me for her.

'Now I would give them some other time, may be next day or may be today itself.' I said to myself.

I called Fazal who was playing with the other children and he came running after hearing her name. We went to our home.

It was already evening and Fazal was on my stomach, jumping and calling out my name to wake up. When I opened my eyes he told me to wake up for some evening snacks. I woke up and he was happy dancing and telling everybody about the news that he had made me waken up. I washed my face and then sat on the chair present nearby. My all cousin were busy in serving the snacks and placing them near to me. I called them all to have it with me. I called my aunt and grandmother too.

While having the snacks grandmother and aunt asked me what I wanted to have in dinner. I didn't want myself to be seen special so I told them anything they wanted.

Next day I woke up early in the morning and when I came out of the room I saw everyone already waken up, I was the last to get up. Fazal was sitting at a corner quietly facing the earth I asked aunt the reason for him to stay like that, then aunt told me that Fazal was asking her everytime to go and make me wake up but she didn't allow him otherwise I would have been waken up much before.

I called him and he came running towards me. We then together brushed and washed our face and sat together to have some breakfast. Then I took him and went to the orchard of litchi. I didn't have much affection for Mango but I like litchi too much. I spent there hours and ate the litchi fruit plucking it directly from the trees. I went to meet with many of the villagers there and now it was noon, I wanted to go home now so I proceeded to home with Fazal.

When I reached home grandfather was already there having lunch, seeing me coming he asked me to join him. I went to have lunch with him. While eating he asked me the duration of stay. I told him that I was going in a day or two.

"So early!! Why? Stay here for some day.", Grandfather asked me for that.

"I wished if I could stay here." I replied.

"But why not? Schools are closed?" Grandfather.

"But coaching isn't." I tried to make him understand.

Grandmother also came running listening my words.

"But stay here for atleast some day. Have the fun of delicious mangoes we have." Grandfather.

"Sorry, grandfather, I couldn't stay here for long." I said.

"OK, then go. But son study seriously, we don't want to interrupt your study." Grandfather.

"Sure, and I know that." I.

I felt very sorry for my grandparents but I had to go for my CUTIE. Here I tried too much to stay alone so that I could easily get into her dream but very rarely I found myself alone, everytime I was surrounded with a number a people and some specially came to see me. Some worker of home and farmland specially came to see me and asked about my mom and father and sister. Only at night I was left alone and that time I lost myself in her dream as much as I could. My grand parents are too soft hearted and so they understood so well and easily. They are the two most beautiful and wonderful people on earth, I know.

I was getting the special treatment there. I was being treated as like a guest or even more than that in my own house. Each and every dish being made was according to my flavor and taste. I also want to be there for some more time but my CUTIE was calling me. I didn't want to leave them so soon, my brother was too happy to have me there and my all cousins too. Fazal didn't allow me to stay alone. Wherever I went he was sure to follow me.

I decided not to get back in just two days but to stay there for two more days atleast if not for too long. My days were brilliant there. I and my all cousins were having fun there. I spent two more days with my cousin and family members.

Now it was the time to departure. I spend there complete four days and then decided to leave for my home, leave for my town, leave for my CUTIE. I wished everyone and went out for the bus stop. My uncle was with me and so was Fazal. They were going to bus stop to see me off. We reached the bus stop and there I got to meet some of the villagers and all were asking me, "why to go so early". They also wished me to continue there for some more time, I told them the reason for going back.

The bus was blowing its horn from far off distance and after a while we could see it coming towards us. I was ready to get inside the bus as soon as it came. It arrived quickly to us and then stopped for the passengers to get inside. I kissed Fazal and wished my uncle and then took a step forward to get into the bus. I acquire a seat there and kept my single bag which was not as heavy as it was at the time of arrival, so I kept it with myself. Now the bus started to move on, Fazal was bidding me a good bye by continuously waving his hands in the air. I wished him back from bus. As the bus moved on to its destination I started to think about the days I spent in my village and all the fun I did with my cousins. It was fabulous.

'How is she now? Did she ever miss me? Did she like me?' All were the question going through my mind.

I kept thinking about her and I thought myself to be very good in that. I completely got lost in her dream. Mentally I was invisible, everytime I thought of her and she made me lost myself. Whenever I thought for her it seemed as if she was with me and that was also the reason why I wished to think of her continually.

As the bus moved on the passenger were getting in making the rush in the bus. Too much rush in the bus but I didn't care, I looked outside the window and made myself lost in her thought. As the bus was getting closer and closer and closer to the destination the rush was getting lessened. I was about to reach to my destination in few minutes.

When I reached to my destination I took my bag with myself and then proceeded to my halt. I went straightaway to my house and then my mother was waiting for me over there. I went inside and mom was ready to have a look at me and suddenly asked the reason to be there so soon. I told her the reason which I told to everyone and also wanted to impress mom by telling her that I was not much comfortable there without her.

In the same evening I called Sahil to ask him if he could company me to the Rajveer's place, and he quickly agreed saying that he too was getting bored when I went away and at that time between five to seven in the evening he considered it to be the most boring time as no one knows what exactly to do at that time.

We went there not to meet Rajveer but to see CUTIE and Rajveer too knew that. Often he said to us, "You rascals were not going to come here daily if Tamannah was not the reason", and we always replied him to be true and taunted him by saying, "What the need to see an asshole like you" and occasionally we burst out. But whenever we went there he always served us with the cold-drink or snacks or sometimes with the homemade drink and snacks.

We reached there and waited for the time for her to leave for home. When the time was close for her to go back we went out on the street and waited for her, after sometimes her rickshaw could be seen coming and I figured her out sitting on the rickshaw with her younger brother. I felt much relaxed after seeing her, as I was much disturbed and my sleeps were taken away by her dream so it was too necessary for me to see her.

After that every day was like same, we went there kicked Rajveer and at the time scheduled for her to return we wait for her and seeing her I relaxed and happily went on to my home from there. It became our daily routine to do with much interest than anything else.

Days were passing as it should be but she was with me everywhere, she didn't let me alone for a single second. She was having the upper hand than every other. I didn't want to know anything but her. I wanted to know everything about her, her likes, dislikes, her aim, her thought for me, how she thinks about her prince charming, her way of seeing the world. Whenever I saw her I got relaxed as if she was the only thing which I would be supposed to do.

Sahil called me to inform that he couldn't come that day in the evening to go to Rajveer's place as he was not well, he had fever and so if I wanted to go then I had to go alone. I told him not to worry but to be fine soon. If Sahil wasn't going then that meant I had to go myself and no one to talk the whole way. I would then be a little bored but anything for her and I must go even if I had to go alone. It was the time for her to go to take tuition I took out my cycle and decided to go Rajveer's place. I proceed towards his house.

While I was about to reach the place or just a yard away from Rajveer's house I saw a classmate in the middle of the road talking with other classmate. I saw them and they saw me coming. I slowed down my cycle to talk with them and to ask about their whereabouts. We wished each other. I asked what did they do the whole holiday, if something new and special but they didn't took their holiday as interesting one as all of us had to continue our coaching and tuitions in the vacation also. No time to do some sort of interesting adventure.

We were having a talk standing on the side of the road keeping my cycle on the roadside. While we were talking I saw a strange thing which I didn't see it till now. I saw my CUTIE. She was coming sitting on her rickshaw. I was talking to my friends but seeing her, I kept quite and kept seeing her thoroughly with my both eyes widely opened.

I was left with a lack of words to talk with the friends. I never thought to see her while going coaching. She was going to coaching to study. I saw her and she also saw me with atleast of five minutes of eye contact with each other. Seeing me dumbstruck all my friends smiled at me.

I was glad to see her as I saw her usually everyday but much glad for the reason to see her infront of me and she also saw me lead to the world of heaven. I went straight to Rajveer's place with much anxiously and impatiently to tell him everything. I speeded up my cycle to be there soon. I reached there and as always he was waiting for us as it was our time to be there. When he opened the door and saw me smiling, he asked the reason for that and also about Sahil. I told him to forget about Sahil and asked him to listen carefully what I was going to narrate.

I narrated everything happened with me while I was coming to his place. I also told him how possessive I felt for her or the time she looked at me. I thought as if the whole world should have stopped at that time, but time was my greatest enemy and it had to fly, and it flew away with its maximum speed it could. I would have passed my whole life staring at her if she looked at me. Each word of narration excited me, just like a little kid after seeing something extra-ordinary. She was someone out of the world for me. Rajveer listened carefully and calmly as a good boy and a good listener and was really happy for me.

Not a single day went by when I didn't go to see my CUTIE and every time I prayed to God that she would also search me in the crowd of the world and every time her eyes should be in search of a face that would be mine. I didn't want to wait for her at the roadside while she goes to her tuition because of the fact that I didn't want to be recognized as a man always staring at her and following her and then she might interpret wrong about me. But I always wanted her to search me, to feel my absence or my presence in the air and its not going to be too easy as later is the case only happened in love and I didn't know till then that whether she completely loved me or not.

Now some more counting days to go and then the school would reopen but these some days were as if like some years for me. As the days went by the exciteness and the eagerness to look at her without any restriction in the class were getting up to the higher level and continued to go up as days were less to go. Everyday was hard to pass. But I knew that if I could handle or pass the summer vacation of some thirty odd days then I was capable to go on for a few more days for her and only for her.

I was very happy for the fewer days to pass but at the same time I expected that these days may pass on quickly.

I went to Rajveer's place for my CUTIE that day. He opened up the door and I went inside. We went upstairs to the roof to have our chat about the school and much about my CUTIE. He was also counting the days when our school was going to reopen. He was also over-excited to meet our friends and above all we didn't do any such kind of mess this vacation at home, so, much anxiously waiting for the mess done at school by us. Now it was time for the CUTIE to return back home. We went downstairs and took up cycle and went to the place where we halt ourselves to see her. We together had a chat at the corner waiting for her putting our eyes on the track, to track her just like a GPS system.

We kept waiting there hoping for her to come.

"Maybe her teacher taught her for more time" said Rajveer looking at me very impatiently and staring at my watch frequently.

"She would be here any time" he whispered again to make me come back to normal.

I kept thinking the reason for her not coming on time. Maybe her tutor is still teaching her, might be she didn't come today, maybe her tuition timing had changed or she might have left the tuition.

We still kept on waiting for her on the road, but it was more than forty-five minutes there for Tamannah. Rajveer asked me to move back to home as it was too late now; he continuously provoked me to move back as if he was in a hurry to go home. I accepted his wordings and was ready to go home but through her place and if I was lucky then I could have a glimpse of her. We bid good bye to each other and then proceeded towards home. I turned my cycle on the way to her home and praying heartily to God to let me see her even if it was for a second only.

I prayed to God all the way to her home. My heart was beating more than a normal speed as I was approaching near to her house. Just a few distances away from her house I slowed down my cycle to have a long time to pass by her house. As I reached much nearer I started searching for her here and there just like a police in search of the criminal.

As soon as I swung my head up towards the sky I was like in heaven, my eyes were stretched and I couldn't see anything except her at that time, my heart had stopped beating and I felt the freshness and coldness even in that hot and hectic season.

And then after a moment, "Booooom!!!!!" I crashed with a pillar along roadside, still my eyes didn't allow me to look anywhere else other than her.

I was like "Wowww" my whole day was converted into the best one and suddenly then I noticed the other two standing by her, one was her brother and the other might be her cousin. I was so happy to see her that I couldn't explain in words.

I woke up early the next day out of excitement and anxiousness for my much awaited wife in the school. Yes, it was the day for the school to re-open. I was very happy deep inside. I reached school half an hour earlier before the due time for the bell to ring up. I knew my CUTIE was always punctual but as a late comer. Punctuality, for her daily visit to the school and late comer, as she reaches school only a minute or two before time.

I wished that she too would come earlier just like me but nothing could be done in such circumstances. Hence I knew that going early couldn't be too much fruitful in context related to her so I went on but a slight less excitedness than others, though it was not true in any sense, I was much more excited than any one else but I didn't want to reveal it out infront of everyone.

I opted the path going through her house to go to the school and I thought that I would get a glance of her gorgeous look for which I was dying.

I reached school seeing too many faces after a long time and all specially from girls side because the boys were always in contact just because of there coaching schedule. I met them all and with my friend but I was waiting for the only one, keeping my eyes on the gate of the class.

She entered into the class after a long wait. I was like out of the real world and I just couldn't keep off my eyes from her. I kept staring at her from the time I saw her without any shyness and hesitation at all. After-all I got this chance after a long time. I repeated my habit of continuously staring at her in class and all else seemed to know it very well.

Hena and Palak usually asked money in her name. They always asked me to give some money as CUTIE wished to have some chocolates. I knew she loved to have 'Dairy-milk' and knowingly Hena asks me out of mischief and I would give her, but later on they asked me money on every second day for her just for fun, even though CUTIE was not demanding and I seemed to knew it very well but anything for her, anything in her name. I felt relieved doing so.

One day I instead of giving them the money bought them the chocolates and asked them to give it to CUTIE. They kept some with them and had given one to her. I knew that they would keep some so I was ready for that. When she took up the chocolate I was too happy as if my whole body and soul was dancing and singing and only I could see it or feel it, cloud nine was the little lower than the place I was on.

Next day in school she reached earlier than I expected. I was with my friend and then Hena called me from behind. I turned back to see her and she handed me the chocolate. I asked her whether it was her birthday. She exclaimed no and told that "CUTIE" had given her to give it to me.

I was short of words at that time to express this happiness. Hena was also smiling seeing me too much happy. I told to tell her thanks in return. She turned to move back to her and then suddenly I asked her to freeze. She turned around sighting for the reason to stop her. I felt a little shy but told her to tell something more to CUTIE along-with the thanks for her chocolate. She asked me what to say more??

I told her to sing a song for her on behalf of me, and the song was………

```
Ye chand sa raushan chehra
Zulfo ka rang sunhara.
Ye jheel si neeli aankhen
Koi raaz ho unme gehra.
Taarif kru kya uski,
Jisne tumhe banaya.
```

Seeing my love and affection for CUTIE, Hena smiled and turned back to go without uttering a single word but she kept a continuous smile on her way back.

My friends were just behind me and as soon as she went they caught me and asked for the treat. I completely denied and then they asked to share the chocolates with them and I never wanted to do this with the first ever thing I got from my loved one. They also knew that so, they asked me to choose between the two. They knew that I would like to go for the earlier one and they would get what they wanted from me.

Anything good to you in love, then be ready to loose up your pocket. Friends are the worms who always suck if you are in love. They will always let you count for the reason for the treat.

Today I decided to ask from any of my friend from girl's side on whom I trust, 'whether I had any chance on her or not? Whether She developed any sort of affinity towards me or not? Whether she liked me or not?' For these queries either Palak or Shalini would be the best for me so I decided to go for both. I reached school on time and then just after that went ahead towards Shalini. She didn't use to come too early but today she was there. I talked to her about things apart from us and then she herself tried to tease me taking the CUTIE's name.

"You are going on the right track." Said Shalini.

"Which track??" I asked her as if I didn't know anything.

"Don't try to be over-smart. Every one knows about you and how crazy and possessive you are for her." Shalini in a teasing mode!!!

"Oh, leave it Nariyal Pani." I tried to tease her back.

I understood what did she mean or was telling about but she didn't want to show it too easily or quickly. Whenever her name was flashed from anyone's mouth or anywhere on paper or blackboard or anything, I got too much excited to talk about her or want that the other person may tell something about her to me, but that too that I didn't want to show my eagerness to talk or listen about her. Here too I tried to do the same and inorder to escape from that situation I teased her back. So, I called her Nariyal paani (coconut water) which I used to say her oftenly because of the fact that she belonged to kerela and coconut is found there in plenty of numbers or you may say more than anywhere in India.

"No- no, really you are on the right path and may be very soon she would respond and accept you and your blooming love for her." Shalini clarifies her side.

"What do you mean by the word soon?? Did she ever tell you about me??" I enquired.

"Not really. But she is always interested in your talks." Shalini.

"What sort of talking?" I enquired again.

"I mean whenever we girls talk to her about you and your mischievous activities, she keenly listened to it just like a small child paying attention to a useful topic." Shalini tried to convince me.

"May I consider it to be her love and affection for me??" I queried like a small baby.

"Yes, you can tell so. She surely has feelings for you, but she might be feeling shy to express it to us." Shalini.

"Yeah!! May be." I.

"But listen, anytime you would be the one to take turn and show the guts to propose her. She is little shy so, no expectations from her side." Ultimately Shalini clarifes my all doubts and gives a Boom to my mind!!!

"Ok! But for that I have to pray a lot to God to give me such strength and guts." I tried to show my inability in this fresh field to her.

"Anyway! But be ready for it and do what you can to gain confidence but be sure you may get that opportunity very soon." Shalini.

"Hope so." I said.

"Good luck." She wished me.

By the time I understood everything she told and gained much of the confidence and was so happy too. Now I got to know that the day would surely arrive on which she would accept me wholly from her heart and mind, but still a long way to go.

'She liked me and I like her too. Isn't it enough to say yes to me by her or did she still want to supervise me more. If she wanted the same then I was ready to give the exam, and let me pass my all friends specially girls, as they did a lot for me.' I thought in my mind.

I got to know from some girls that they always keep chanting my name as a student everyone would appreciate for Excellency, brilliancy, soft behaviour, honest, helpful and every sort of good words from dictionary to describe me infront of her.

Days were passing quickly and I was getting progressed in love, everything was going fine. Yash came to me and started talking to me. He was a good friend but not as good as my buddies and Yash was also like other as a friend. We chatted a little and suddenly he jumped into my personal life. Yeah! I knew my personal life was around Tamannah and was no longer a personal as everyone knew about me and my strong affinity for her.

"My friend may I tell you something?" Yash questioned.

"Yeah, ofcourse. Tell what you want." I answered.

"Listen, I know you are very much passionate about Tamannah and deeply into her love." Yash halted for a while.

"Yes, then what happened?" I asked him in a very pathetic mode.

"You are a good guy so I decided this to tell it you." Yash.

"Ok! But tell me what you mean and please complete your words." I asked him with full curiosity and my heart was beating with the speed more than a normal.

"Actually yesterday I saw Tamannah talking with a boy after dismissal right infront of the college gate and was giving him a gift." He clarifies.

"Who was that boy?" I questioned him back.

"I don't know who he was". He answered.

"How you didn't know?" I counter- questioned him.

"Yes, truly I don't know him; he was an outsider and specially came to meet her." He replied.

"Ok, then fine." I responded.

"That's why I want you to be at a safer distance from her and not to be cheated by her and that is the reason why I told you everything, I didn't want that you might be depressed after reaching the target and not achieving it." Yash again tried to give weight over his words.

I didn't respond towards him at this time and slowly went ahead and far from him. I knew Yash from my childhood that he would never ever try to cheat me to give any false information but I had too much of love in my heart for my CUTIE and an unworthy trust on her that I could deny anyone's words and reject anyone's talks against her.

May be Yash had seen so but it might be possible that he didn't understand or knew correctly about what he told me.

I knew that everything we saw with our eyes isn't true. I didn't even bother about to think for a second about what Yash told me. I had a blind faith on my CUTIE. I didn't even try to remind his wordings. I knew her and by then her behaviour was not untouched by me. She was a pure girl. I would never think such things about her even in my dreams what Yash did display in the reality.

She is more than my love, my life. She is my reason to survive, my reason to live for, the reason to be happy, the reason to study, the reason to be a good person. Everytime I looked at her, I got a strong desire to talk to her, to keep looking at her but neither a single talk neither from her side nor from my mine.

It was more than a tragedy for me as I spoke to everyone in my class except her. Not a single girl was there with whom I didn't talk. Now it was more than six months looking at her but didn't get the courage to take up a chance.

'Mantasha' was her closest friend, I believed, and also a new comer just like her, but I spoke to her quite frequently, but I don't know what happened to me while talking to Tamannah. Mantasha didn't even know me much better than any of the girls but still she was very helpful to me. Many a time I asked Mantasha about her and everytime she responded like an intellectual person keeping the ball always in her court.

Today too I asked her.

"Why doesn't your friend talk to me, just as u talk??" I questioned to her.

"She will talk very soon." She answered.

"Keep going with your hard work. She murmured in my ear."

After she told me, I smiled a little and thought to ask her the question that I asked to Shalini and knew that she is the closest to her and she may and must know what no one knows. So, I decided to go for it.

"Ok. Now tell me did she ever talk about me with you or anyone?" I further enquired after a small break.

"Actually she is a little shy by the nature so a really bad question as she really feels too shy to talk about a guy or to express the feeling for him." Mantasha bowled me with her delivery.

"Ok-Ok!! Do you think she likes me??" I smiled and asked.

"Go and ask from her the same." She again punches me back with a smile on her face.

She didn't answer me clearly but I guess something good for me in her smile which Mantasha passed me while I asked her.

There was naughtiness in Mantasha's smile which told me that good days are not too far or may be they would arrive soon.

Next day in school Palak came to me and asked me that when was I going to propose CUTIE. I told her that I didn't even think to propose.

"So do you love to live without her empty handed?" She hit me with her words.

"Hey! Be calm." I tried to normalise her.

"Why bro? Why don't you approach her?" She asked.

"Actually I didn't plan it till now." I said.

"What are you waiting for?" She continually bowled me.

"Palak, I don't even know whether she loves me or not, and what if she rejected me. I showed her my point of view."

"No, She would never reject you." Palak added.

"How could you be so confident over that!!!" I asked.

"I can because I know she too loves you." Palak said confidently.

"What?" I exclaimed with joy.

"Yes, I know she loves you though she never told this to anyone of us." Palak said.

"Then how could you say so??" I asked with too much of eagerness.

"Because whenever we girls talked to her about you she always smiled and listened with too much of attention." Palak.

"Ok. That's fine but whenever she would tell anyone that she loves me then only I would propose her." I put forward my thought.

"Ok. We would try." She whispered and went away with a smile on her face.

Let me clear you one thing that I didn't have any intention to propose her only after I knew she loves me but the main reason behind telling so to Palak was that, that from then onwards she along with the girls will try to let Tamannah say that 'yes, I love Lucky'. And then I would know the answer when I would propose her and it would be a little easy for me to gather all courage to propose her.

Days were progressing and so my love story. Upto then I decided to write a Shayari or poetry for her and give it to her indirectly. I tried too hard to write but didn't get the right words and a write place, but finally I managed to compile my own Shayari for her. I handed over that to Palak and asked her to read aloud and let Tamannah listen this shayari.

She did exactly the same. Tamannah was too happy after listening to the words and I could easily see the smile on her face that long lasted. While handing over the shayari to Palak I kept on gazing at Tamannah for her reaction after the listening completely to the shayari and then I could see that on my CUTIE's face. She was continuously smiling with a shyness on her face and the shyness grew me more as the girls started teasing her by my name many times for the shayari made by me for her.

Now I was sure that I was being liked by her and it was enough for me to be happy. My friend Sahil, Rajveer and Aakash all knew it. The same day Mantasha talked to me and asked me that when was I going to propose her, I ignored her and further told her that when I get to know that she loves me then only I would propose her and very soon may be some day I could tell her so.

She asked me not to bother by her response but do approach her directly by proposing her and I knew that she likes you. Startled and my mouth was wide opened to tell something but couldn't. I couldn't believe on my ears what I have heard just then. I asked her again and again to repeat again what she told just now and everytime she clarifies my doubt and told that she loved me. Now I had a lot of things to tell and ask.

"Really! She loves me??" I asked in a joy.

"Yes, dumbo." Mantasha said in a teasing manner.

"Surely!" I.

"Oh God! You are really an asshole. Yes, yes, yes." Mantasha.

"Then why didn't you ever tell me this before whenever I asked you?" I.

"Because till that time I too didn't know that she loved you or not, but today I could say that being confirm and confidently." Mantasha.

"Did she ever tell you about this?" I eagerly asked.

"Not directly." Mantasha.

"I could easily see love for you in her eyes." Mantasha added.

"Are you sure that she would accept my proposal." I.

"Yes, without any hesitation I could say so." Mantasha.

"Thank you very much for supporting me morally." I.

"No need to say thank you and if you are really thankful to me so go and tell straight away everything to Tamannah and tell her what is going in your heart." Mantasha.

"I am a new comer in this field so I don't know when and what and how to tell." I.

"Simply go and express your feelings and after then you would be an experience holder." Mantasha.

"Tell me when are you going to propose her?" Mantasha added.

"May be some day very soon." I.

"No, not any day but today itself. She is waiting very impatiently for your proposal." Mantasha.

"Is it like that?" I.

"Obviously." Mantasha.

"Are you going?" She added.

"Please give me sometime to plan or think for that." I.

"You are really mad. She is waiting for you and you are making her counting days for you." Mantasha expressed her anger.

"I am not making her counting days. Today, itself I got to know that she loves me." I.

"You idiot, how could you know it before asking her, it is only the kindness of God and a positive thing that you know it now." Mantasha.

"Having known everything then also you are showing your laziness in taking action." She was onto me and was forcing me continuously to propose her.

She added then, "Go and propose her, she is in the class."

"Please-Please, leave it for today. May be some other day I could ask her." I refused to go.

"Too slow in taking action, such a dumbo!!" Mantasha.

She went away saying so and I kept on memorising what she told me. Back to home in the evening from school and coaching I started thinking what happened with me in the school.

Everyone came to me and urged me and forced me even to propose Tamannah. I couldn't understand why were they so excited? Why were they taking much of their interest in that? I thought much about Mantasha and her words. Whatever she told wouldn't be without any logic. She was the closest to my CUTIE at that time and if she wants me to propose her best friend then their might be some truth in her words blushed before me. She never ever talked to me in such a manner as today, may be she was suggested or advised by Tamannah to tell that to me as I was making the day too longer.

Now there was a satisfaction in my heart but whenever I thought about Tamannah or took her name, my heart gets pumped up everytime out of the intolerable happiness and I just wanted to shout aloud her name in joy.

I was thinking on the day on which I would propose her that if this is the situation of mine at the present time, just by knowing that she loves me, then what would happen when she would respond to my proposal in a positive manner, she would overcome her shyness and accept my love infront of everyone. Maybe I would go mad or left the world out of too much happiness and excitement. All sort of thoughts were running in my mind and they pleased me a lot, but I was on the case of dilemma on how to approach her and what to tell?

Now it was more than a week after Mantasha and Palak asked me to propose her. Someone or the other used to advice me everyday to propose her, but I couldn't get the courage to talk on that topic with Tamannah.

One day at the lunch time while I was about to leave the class and was going out towards the canteen Hena called me loudly from the class. I turned back and upto then she was only a feet away.

"Yes, what happened?" I.

"I needed to ask something from you." Hena.

"Yes, ask." I.

"Are you waiting for any occasion?" Hena.

"I didn't get you, what you wanna say." I.

"Don't run your empty brain on what I told." Hena.

"Then what are you saying?" I.

"I was just thinking that you might be waiting for something good to happen and then you would go and grab a chance to propose her." Hena.

Now I came to know what she meant to say. Day by day almost each girl from my class had come and asked me to propose her. They all seemed to be much more excited than me.

"Oh! That's your point." I.

"And your point?" Hena asked me with a slight anger.

"Listen, I know that she loves me but I didn't ever listen her telling openly to you girls that she loves me." I said in a confusing manner however I was sure that Tamannah loved me, it was all to escape from them.

"Oh! Now you want us to force her anyhow to say that she loves you" Hena.

"No-no I don't want you to force her, but I just want that, it to listen it with my own ears only." I.

"Ok, we would do this too for you." Hena.

She left me telling to be ready to propose.

'I don't know why they all are showing too much of interest in my personal life?' I said to myself.

On the very next moment I was surrounded by five girls and they all came to clarify the doubt what Hena had told them right then. I nodded my head in positive response. Palak said that she would get to listen those three words from her mouth very soon but not directly infront of me rather them.

Next day as the bell rang for the lunch and the students started going out of the class for the lunch, Hena called me to keep my ears on the girl's side. I saw almost all the girls teasing Tamannah and forcing her to tell that she loves me, but Tamannah was smiling shyly.

Hena then asked her boldly so that I could hear what she was asking. She asked her that does she love me and after a while she told yes with a smile on her face. I listened it clearly and saw it also, CUTIE was unaware that it was the master play of Hena and their entire group to let me listen that with CUTIE's own mouth and yes they succeeded.

I was too much relieved listening to that but I didn't tell it to my friends, I wanted it to keep it a secret from them until I proposed her. All the girls after that came to me and congratulated me and then immediately asked for the treat. I denied and told them to give it only after I proposed her and so they were forcing me to do it today itself. I also had a strong desire to propose her but didn't know what actually happened when I planned and thought of doing that actually.

A few days passed and everyone was forcing me to tell Tamannah directly that I love her. That day just after the dismissal I was on the ground talking with Palak and Hena and then suddenly Mantasha arrived and joined us.

As expected we all were talking about Tamannah. I was asking them the tips to propose her and they keep telling me why to hesitate so much.

Seeing this Mantasha got angry and scolded me saying "She is in love with you fucking asshole and everytime she is waiting for you very impatiently, that might be today that you should propose her, but you are passing days only. Will you propose her in your this birth itself?"

I didn't utter a word at that moment and was stubbed there like a statue saying nothing. I said to myself in my mind that 'don't say anything to her at this time as she was a hot ball of fire at the moment and it would hit me again and again if I say anything.'

I just said I don't know what to tell. On that she blushed on me and showed her angriness and said that I had to propose her today itself anyhow otherwise she wouldn't talk to me from the next day.

She threatened me and over that Palak and Hena supported. It was beyond expectation as they were always on my side in the whole nine years of schooling. They too threatened me by the same words as that of Mantasha. They were forcing me to propose her anyhow.

Mantasha went away from us and returned back very soon. I dropped my all weapons infront of the girls as I too was very excited and keen to do that. I was waiting for that day to arrive soon and lately and lastly it had come. I told them 'Ok I would do that today itself.'

I asked Mantasha that where was my CUTIE as I didn't find any trace of her. She replied that Tamannah was in the class and she had just left her there telling to wait for me as I was going to talk to her for my life.

They asked me to get inside but I was hesitating a little. They pushed me from back and let me to go close to the class. While reaching to the class I saw Tamannah standing and waiting for me. No one else was there in the class except her, as if the whole class was emptied only for us. I reached inside the class. As soon as I reached into the class I opened my mouth to tell, but then Mantasha interrupted me by saying.

"Let us go first!!".

I didn't utter a word at Mantasha rather I waited for all of them to go. I was dying out of shyness.

They all went out of the class but not too far, they were standing right on the gate keeping their ears inside to listen, what I was about to tell. I saw here and there and then my eyes got stuck on her face. I had a lot to say but not even a word was coming out. As I was thinking and wishing the whole world to stop at that moment.

I kept seeing her but her eyes were as if discovering something on the floor. I was continuously staring at her and she to the floor. She didn't even try to look at me a single time. I just moved my eyes away from her knowing that the time would not be enough to pass on like that. So I decided to tell now for what I was there.

"I…. I LOVE…. I LOVE YOU."

I expressed my feelings before her.

"Do you love me?" I asked her in a very eager way.

And then over Tamannah replied "I don't know!!".

"Do you love me?". I asked her again.

When she said that she didn't know the answer of that question and she was confused that does she love me or not. But I knew that it was her shyness which didn't allow her to clear my path in the very first go or to express her feelings in a single time. So I decided to ask her again.

"Don't know!!", She replied again with the same answer.

"Tamannah I really love you!!! Do you?" Now at this time I asked her with full of my affection and emotions as I was willing to listen yes from her mouth.

This time she understood me that how serious I was for her and then she replied "YES!!!!!".

As soon as she replied Yes to me she went away from the class out of shyness and didn't want to face me any more right there.

She left and all the girls present there were smiling at me as if I had won a battle and they were there to welcome me with a smile. One of them was so happy and excited as if she had received the question paper before the exam…!!!

For me it was just like any dream that I proposed any girl for the first ever time and it got accepted. I was like in the seventh world, it seemed like everything had stopped for a moment I was continuously staring at the gate from where Tamannah left the class. My friends too were standing over there but I couldn't find a sight of them. I was just lost.

My all friends were calling me to come out of the class but I couldn't even hear them nor could I see them. For me I was still at that moment when Tamannah was at the gate with a shying smile on her face, keeping her head down and moving out by escaping from her friends. Everything slowed down slowly and I could grab each and every moment and captured it in my eyes.

I was slowly getting seated on the bench and my friends were getting in with a smile and a slight shout which I could only feel. Then after a moment one of my friend stabbed me from the back and I was shocked as if something uneven happened just in a second, but it wasn't so they were there infront of me for a long time, instead I was not in my conscious.

Now I was back into the real world after rooming around in my minds happiness. My all friends screamed and asked for the treat at sudden. I was there sitting on the bench and smiling and didn't no anything to what to speak. I just nodded my head and asked them to move to the canteen. I gave them the treat there, they all were teasing and congratulating me for my new life which I would start with my CUTIE.

Then now when I reached at home I started thinking what had happened with me. While having my food I was stuck at that moment and my mother continuously reminded about my food. I was like out of the world and was so happy. It was 11th Sept that day and it was Tuesday, I couldn't forget that day, it was the happiest day of my life and I think I was the happiest person at that day on the earth. I was very eagerly waiting for the next day to come.

Here the next day arrived, I was at the school and all of my friends and classmates were passing a very weird smile to me, it seemed by their smile that they have known everything about me. All were staring at me as I had got something very precious.

Yeah! She was the most precious for me, but eyeing on some one and if you are the one of whom all were noticing then it sounds too much awkward and you would not be feeling comfortable at that time. I had really got a gemstone in my life. She was most precious stone in the collection of my precious and the secret treasure. God had given me the best gift ever.

Not only the batch mate but also my junior seemed to know all. Some of the junior always passed a smile seeing me and some of them came directly to me and asked for the treat. Somehow I managed to get a narrow escape.

I proposed her, she accepted it, all was good but one thing continually made me to think was that I or we never had a talk till that time. Would it be like that always or we had to take a step ahead and then try to conversate in the class or if not that, then on the mobile. It didn't happen a single time in the whole seven to eight months that we had ever talked except on the day of my birthday for just a single liner talk, and then after we remained speechless infront of each other and now we are together.

But talking was must important for me now and I had to tell her also or do something or should try to approach her in the class first by leaving all my shyness and inconveniency back at home. Many of our common friends also knew it and so they too wanted us to start talking in the class for anywhere where we could talk.

On the same day when I was in the class I tried not to stare at CUTIE oftenly because of the reason that, the previous day I had proposed her and almost everyone knew it and my staring would be a moment to rejoice for others. Everyone's eyes were on us so, I looked at her hardly that day. While on lunch time when I was on the ground with my friends and all of them were teasing me, I just turned my head around out of shyness and then I saw Palak and Hena and many of the girls standing at a corner and signaling me to come over there.

I obeyed their order just like an obedient boy and reached there. No sooner did I reach there, they too started teasing me.

'Everybody, see the smile on his face'. Hena started.

'I always keep smiling'. I.

'Yeah! But it is the smile of some happiness'. Palak.

'Happiness, no-no babes'. I.

'Yeah bro! your face is glittering like it was never before'. Palak.

'Ok; jokes apart. Aren't you happy'? Palak.

'I am'.

'How was your day yesterday'? Ankita.

'Better than ever, and I could never forget yesterday in my entire life'.

'Tamannah told us something today'. Palak.

'What did she told'? I.

'She had a serious complain':; Hena.

'What complain'?

Tamannah told us that, before you proposed her, you used to stare at her everytime, but today, just a single day after you proposed, you hadn't even looked at her a single time. Palak.

I burst into laughter and then realized my CUTIEs cuteness. That's why she is CUTIE. What a cute complain she had about me. Her cuteness made me fall in love more and more.

Till then my friends abused aloud at me and then I left.

As soon as the dismissal bell rang Mantasha asked me to wait. After all the fellow mates rushed back to their home, she called me to follow her. I followed her and then she told me to get inside a junior class. I asked the reason but she didn't respond to any of my question.

I went inside and saw Tamannah standing in class. Now I understood Mantasha's intention in sending me to that class.

She wanted that both of us should spend time together and talk to each other. May be that, class was on the corner of the school and no one was their, that's why Mantasha might have chosen that for us. I salute those girls who did a lot to me for those meets.

I went inside and stood right infront of Tamannah. She slowly looked up at me and then put her head down and looked the floor. I talked to her of where about and then told what Palak told me at the lunch time regarding the complaint.

She was smiling too cozy and denied. I asked her whether, she was afraid of me and then she said "no" to that then, I asked her to tell me directly what she had to or what complaint she had for me. She again smiled. Her smile was mind blowing. She looked like a heavenly angel. I wanted her to smile forever and I would keep staring at her for my whole life.

It was so attractive that if she had asked me my life there while smiling, I would have given that for her.

I was so happy at that moment that I couldn't believe myself that, I was talking to her. It seemed like any dream to me. I wished that someone would pinch me and make me realise that I was in the real world. I never got a chance to talk to her ever before, but now she was mine and I was hers, and then we could talk.

I had really waited a long time for this day. I wanted to continue more, but it was the very first experience of both to talk with their loved ones and we both were feeling shy and were short of words to communicate with each other.

Everytime I asked her something, she solemnly looked up and again got stuck to the floor and then she answered or told anything. Her extreme shyness would have killed me if, I had stayed there for more time. I was a big fan of my loved ones till then and also her cute smile.

It was our first conversation so we both didn't kne,w what to tell or how to respond or, what to ask and that was the only reason behind that we got out too early from the class.

When I got out of the class I was shocked as I saw Mantasha along with Palak, Hena, Ankita and Vidya, all were standing by the gate to welcome me by there naughty smile.

Palak asked "What happened inside?" and I said that, nothing except a few talk, and then she further proceeded with her question that what talks were those and I was strictly ordered not to give the excuse by saying that it was quite personal.

I told her what had happened. I didn't want to stay there with the girls for even a second because I knew them, they would tease me and laugh at me always but, they still loved me and it was their right to do so as, they had helped me a lot. But I didn't want to get teased, so I just escaped from them. I proceeded back to my home.

On the way back to the home only CUTIE was in my mind. She always dominated my mind and not a single time was there, when her thought was on the lowest floor of a ten storey building. She was always on the top of my mind. Her home was on the way to my home and did work just similar to the work what oxygen did in the burning.

My heart beat only for her. I tried to pass my day being lonely at home so that, I would get more time to think of her, to be lost in her.

I wanted to talk to her but how, we hardly get any time in school and that was also for not more than five minutes. I was too desperate to talk to her but I didn't have her number. Might be she too was suffering from the same situation.

Next day in school when the girls left us alone in our class to talk I went close to her and asked her the number on which we could talk. She dictated me her number and I immediately asked her the time at which she would be free. She replied me to call her at anytime I wished to.

We did talk a little at that time but I was much excited to talk to her on the phone.

One thing I must say here that if, I wanted then I could have easily made her to talk to me in the class, ground, canteen anywhere, but I didn't want it to happen too easily as, I also felt little shyness in approaching her and secondly, I didn't want anyone to point a finger on her, that, before being in relation she was too shy to talk with anyone, and now she is spending her most of the time with me so quickly. And moreover I didn't knew what to talk. If we would try talking in class then more than eighty percent of the time we would spend simply standing and being speechless. It was the hesitation or you can say that shyness was still with me.

In the evening I called her around 7 pm, she picked up the phone at the other end. We wished good evening to each other and then exchanged some more words. There on the phone too we were short of words and she was more than me. She was actually in a mute mode everytime. She didn't say anything. The only time when she forced her mouth to give a exercise was when, I asked her something and that too, in a brief. Her response was always like 'Yes', 'No', or 'Don't no'. She didn't say anything except those three words. We were in a silent mode normally so I decided to be apart from such situation. So I decided to hung-off the phone but before hanging off the phone we exchanged those three magical words 'I LOVE YOU' and she responded back as 'I LOVE YOU TOO'.

We hardly talked for more than ten minutes. I knew it to be too early to cut the phone, but it was good for us. I would try to enlarge the conversation time gradually, rather than on the initial days as both of us would have thought it to be too lengthy and a little awkward as we were on silent mode thoroughly. I believed that, once we felt comfortable with each other then, we would continue long chat without any supplement of our friends. Till today we were on the kindness and helpfulness and mercy of our friends who let the class empty to make us talk to each other.

Days were passing and my love life was also going through very smoothly. We did talk in school with the help of our common friends and everyday I rang up and had a talk for the short time. The duration of the call was still the same, it hadn't increased, but then too I was satisfied as I believed "something is better than nothing".

Everyday in class I looked at the CUTIE most of the time. She felt shy and that's why she never tried to sit infront, rather on the corner of the second bench as I always looked at her being parallel to her on the opposite row. Upto then I only looked at her but also wanted her, to look at me at the same time. So I started telling her friend sitting on the same bench to call her and as soon as CUTIE turned around we had an eye contact and couldn't remove it as my heart didn't gave me permission to excuse my eyes.

Everytime someone had to pinch me to pay attention to the studies in the class. And at that time she straight away turns her face to the blackboard in shy. Seeing her I felt too much relaxed and now then, it had became my habit. Everytime I tried to find an eye on her and wanted to get lost in that.

I always was in touch with the girl sitting next to her so that she may give an space and allow me to see my CUTIE. All the girls those who used to sit next to CUTIE got disturbed that, where the hell, I have arrived from to hit them on their butt every-time? But not a single time they complaint me about my habit but they seemed to be enjoying it. I asked them more than five to ten times to shift a little in a period of forty-five minutes.

In the earlier days I had to tell them to get back but quickly, they got trained and after that as soon as I saw them, they pushed themselves back to let us see each other. I was always very much desperate for the dismissal of the school and was waiting impatiently to talk to her face to face.

As soon as the bell rang for the dismissal I kept waiting outside for everyone to leave the class but then itself, Mantasha called me to follow her and this time she took me to the junior class in the corner of ground. She asked me to get inside as CUTIE was already waiting there.

I went inside close to CUTIE and kept standing there and just exchanged a few words. Meanwhile we were talking there, a female sweeper arrived and we were completely unaware of that. She looked at us and went away.

We too came outside. I told Palak that they should have atleast signaled us that, someone was arriving when she asked the reason to come out of the class so early. She told us to relax and not to worry as she wouldn't tell anyone. We were relaxed then and I then left for home.

She wouldn't tell it to any higher authority but she would share it among her co-worker and also the member of school management.

The school management staff knew me very well so he warned me and hide the situation from any other person and signalled me to be a sincere student and to leave what I was doing.

He never told me directly but, I understood his point of view and what it meant. From then onwards I was more conscious towards my love life.

After that almost every teacher who taught us have known our relation but never tried to tell a single word to any of us.

Two months passed on happily. Our love life was on the right track. Till then we started talking to each other in the class too. We meet in school not like any stranger, but like the loved ones. We talked in the school and in the home too via calls, we were both happy having each other. She made my life too good to thought before.

She was my dream and it had come true. Having her, I had a reason to smile and to be happy.

We talked in the evening for a while and then after I got a call from my village, grandma was on the call. She asked me the plan about EID that year whether, to visit there or not? and EID was scheduled in the same month.

We did every festival basically in our home town and very rarely we went to the village. This time grandma asked and wished that, if we could be there at this festival to celebrate together and spend the charmness of EID altogether.

My Mom told us that we didn't have any plan for the village but we could make it if she wished so. I too had a talk with my grandma on the phone. After that my mom connected the call to Dad and told him everything. My dad is a noble person and would try everything that could make his parents and my grandparents happy and pleased. So, he decided to go along with all of us. And also we didn't celebrate any of the festival in the village since last seven to eight years. So it was not the bad decision to go there anyway. It was all my parents thought.

But how could I be willing to go leaving CUTIE alone. She was my life till then. I couldn't bear the pain of separation for a week. She was on my top priority list. I tried to convince my father, as I knew if he would understood then no need to ask mom. He would tell her, but my father took it as a turn to make me understand contrary to my expectation. I put my head down to turn onto his knees and understood that, I would have to go anyhow.

I did want to tell this truth to CUTIE that, I would not be available for her in school or in town for the reason that I was moving to my village for a week. But I didn't gather the courage to tell her or it might be a little thing to be worried for her so no need to tell. I would tell her on the day when I reached there.

I tried to spend the day normally and didn't let anyone, to know that was going inside me. I was calm from outside but was too much worried about Tamannah.

How could I live without her all the week? I wouldn't get much time to call her when I would reach there. No daily meeting, nothing. I was worried a lot taking this condition in my mind.

The calmness on my face was the sign of forth- coming thunder and the wailings of the tides. These thunder and the tides inside me drowning me into it. I was in a huge dilemma. What to do then?

On the last day of my school before going to the village while I was talking to Mantasha I told her accidentally. It was a slip of tongue. She then told that to Tamannah and then she became angry and sad as I wouldn't be with her for some day, but much angry for the reason that I hadn't told her directly before she got to knew by her friend. I tried to make her understand. She was very soft cornered so, she forgave me and lost her anger very soon.

From then I knew the fact that everything happening or, going to happen must be known to her. She had the right to ask and know my each and everything related to my personal life as now it wasn't only mine, it belonged to her too.

I was waiting for the dismissal to have some more talk with her. Soon after dismissal we started talking about my departure. When to go? How many days to spend there? When to return back? How to be in contact?

I had to give all her answers and also I assured her to call her from there, but also I made her aware of the inconveniency to call her at everytime. Before leaving for home she took out her ring from her ring finger which she always used to wear and handed it to me.

I asked her that, what was that? She asked me to take it with me so that whenever I would be thinking about her I could see that ring and feel her presence. It was too filmy and also it showed how loving and caring my CUTIE was. I took it from her and kept it with myself. She then smiled and asked me to return it when I would come back.

I obeyed her and started laughing together as it seemed to be quite filmy!! I bid her good bye and asked her to take care of herself and then we left for our home. I took the ring and wore it in my finger with all my love and kept it caring the whole day.

Next day morning around 9 am we proceeded towards our village. It took more than four hours to reach there. There wasn't a single second on the way that she was away from my thought. I always got lost in her dreams and kept on thinking that, how difficult it would be to spend those days without her. I was missing her too badly. And then suddenly my cell phone rang, I took it out to receive the call.

The number displayed on the screen revealed that it belonged to my home town as the code was represented there. I picked up the call. A cute and a lovely sound stuck into my ears. It was she, she was there on the phone. She was on the other side of the call. Yes, she called me. I thanked God to listen my wish and respond over that.

The fate too wanted that we should be together. I was just thinking about her and I got a call from her. It was a shocking surprise for me, I couldn't believe on my ears.

We had a very little talk as I had to keep the phone because, I was surrounded by the family. I was too happy. She called me from the P.C.O. outside our school. I was sad too as, I couldn't spend much time on phone with her.

We had a talk, though it was too short but it doesn't matter for me as I always gave importance to the intention of the people and it was her true intention and love. I told her that we were about to reach in an hour or two and would message her as soon as I reach there.

Finally we reached there, placed our luggage and I made myself busy in messaging her text. All got busy in talking to each other. I went inside a room and started talking with the ring she gave me. I kissed that ring many times.

The house was filled with 20 people, but I was feeling too lonely being away from her. Everytime I missed her, I kissed the ring which made me think that she was present there with me. Her presence in my life meant everything to me. She made my life meaningful and a reason to live and enjoy the life.

I called her everyday and talked with CUTIE, though the call was for the short duration but it satisfied my heart. I didn't find myself alone in numbers as everytime there was someone who surrounded me. Very hardly I stole the time for her. Everyone was happy there except for me. EID was yet to be celebrated but I wanted the week to wrap up soon.

It was the day of the celebration. Finally the day arrived for which I was waiting a lot as, I would I ask my parents to return as soon as EID arrived. I did exactly the same. I started asking the day from my father on which we would return back to our hometown. I told him that my school and coaching went missing. He then agreed to go after a day.

I spent the day there seeing and kissing the ring and only thinking about her. The week was so hectic for me as I didn't even had a glance of her and I couldn't wait long so, I had to make the excuse and convince dad to move back soon.

I was in my home back in my hometown. I reached there after two days from EID. I missed my relative from the village but missed my CUTIE more than anything. I was very passionate to get her view live. I called her to give her the good news. She picked up the phone and then we continued the talk. I told him how badly did I miss her and she too expressed that she too missed me a lot. I told her, if she too missed me so badly as I? Then there should be a kiss to enjoy the moment of being together after sometime, to part away the strain of separation, I said.

She smiled and said that, if I wanted a slap from her. I told her that I didn't need a slap, rather a kiss would be great. She again said to slap me if continued that talk again. After so long time she was in the mood after I went to village.

I went to school the next day before time as I prayed to God to let her see while going to school on the way, but I didn't find her. In the school I kept waiting for her and after a while there she was.

A long lasting smile went through my face and she too smiled. We were in the class and were having a talk with each other. Days were short and happy but the night were sleepless.

It was winter and cold wind was blowing which, intensified the winter. In a week we arrived to school much before time for a day or two to spend sometime together without any interruption of our classmates.

It was also the day I called her before time. She reached and then we talked a bit. After that we started moving together in some other class. We went to a class which was much inside than any other class and in that chilling, windy winter also we could feel the warmth there.

We stayed there a little and talked also. We were too close to each other. Gradually the distance between us got shortened and after that our body was touching each other.

I don't know it was us who filled the gap between, or the earth was shrinking towards us which made us to move closer to each other.

In no moment she was into my arms. I felt if, my goose bumps. I had never felt this before. We were opposite to each other. I looked into her eyes but she felt shy and her eyes was stuck to the ground. I wanted to feel her more so I placed my hand around her belly a little tight. She came too close to me. Our eyes and heads were in the downward position.

We didn't call or tried to call or talk to each other. We got more closer and closer and a moment came where, I could feel her warm breath. Gap between us was then completely filled.

Gradually our lips got in contact and then everything got blurred infront of me, all I could see was her face and then

I closed my eyes. We then exercised our lips on each other. She enjoyed that moment. Her eyes were closed and she left herself into my arms loosing her body as if she had devoted herself to me.

I wanted that, the period might be longer as it could. I wanted to feel her more and the time to stop flying. I had Goose Bumps.

Exercise of lips went for a few seconds and it seemed that we were attached with each other for hours and then suddenly a shock went through us as if, we were hit by any lightening bolt and then we aparted from each other.

I looked at her and she looked back at me. Our eyes were glittering and were shining back to each other in joy. There was satisfaction and lot of happiness in her eyes, I could clearly make that out. She was the girl I had ever kissed and I always wanted to kiss her only. It was my first ever kiss.

Whole day in the school, I was happy and was lost in her thought and the deed that happened, everytime that moment went through my mind in the slow motion and made me more happier. Time to time the morning scene get reminded itself into my mind. I was too happy to be noticed.

Kaveri Mishra asked me why I was so happy and I told her that I always keep smiling and there's no other reason for my happiness.

When I called her in the evening then after some time of talking I asked her about the morning that, whether she liked it or not? Was it good or not? Was she satisfied or not? All of the first she was full of hesitation and was out of shyness but then after a moment she replied back in a positive way. She made my day, and I too was satisfied to have a girl like her in my life and also we were having good days together.

In the early morning assembly it was announced that the school is organizing a trip to Bodh Gaya in Bihar on most probably on coming Saturday and for the extra info related to the tour we were asked to consult to our class-teacher. We all were very excited to go for the tour.

When we asked our teacher he also confirmed it and said that the students above class four and those interested could give their names to the respective class teacher latest by Thursday. We all guys started talking about the trip and our willingness to go. Everyone asked one or the other whether they are going or not.

In my class of sixty students almost 50 of them were willing to go. I too together in my group wished to give our names on the same day to the teacher but then the thought ran into my mind and I just changed my mind to first consult it with our parents and want their consent for the trip and moreover I wanted Tamannah too to come with us for the tour. So, it would always better to have a talk on the issue.

I reached home and talked about the trip with my mother and then to my father on the phone. My father always wanted me to join some educational tour whenever organized and everytime he granted me the permission to go.

This time too he was with my expectations and gave me the permission. I then talked to my CUTIE in the evening on the topic and she showed her inconveniency to come up. I asked her the reason, o'er that she replied that her parents would never allow her to go anywhere on tour.

My heart got dipped and felt quite sad, also I was messed up with the situation as my parents allowed me to go but I couldn't go for the trip without my CUTIE. I became restless and didn't want to go without my CUTIE. I completely made my mind not to go on the trip and if ever then with her by my side.

Next day when I reached school all kept asking me to come and I kept on ignoring them. All the girls in the class asked me whether to come or not as they were in full confidence that I would surely go because of the fact that I had never ever missed any of the educational tours from the school whenever organized since class first. So they were more hopeful for me.

Whenever my friends asked me the reason, I would tell them the truth and from there on they started insisting me to go with them and I kept refusing. They made me assure that they would have a talk with Tamannah and would surely force her to come. But when they had a talk with my CUTIE, then she explained her problem to them that why she couldn't come.

My friends knew it very well that I wasn't going for the tour without my CUTIE. They gave the name including me without giving any information to me. When I got to know it I asked the explanation and they kept numb. Later on they all said "Ok friend we too are not going if you aren't". Then I was in a huge mess. I was completely confused that what to do and what not to. I kept thinking all about the friends and CUTIE too. Then I talked again to my CUTIE and pleaded her to come but she couldn't get the permission as she told me earlier.

Next day I reached back to school with a decision to go with friends for their happiness. I knew them, they were all totally mad and I had to do what they were willing to as I could not hurt them too. It was the decision I made from my mind without concerning with the heart. I made up my mind to go for the trip inorder to see my friends happy, I knew that I wouldn't be happy at all on the whole tour as I would be completely missing my CUTIE, but yet I decided to go to keep my friends happy.

My friends, after knowing my decision came to me and made me understand all about the life, saying

"Bro someone you hate, hate for life time. Someone you dislike, dislike for life time. And someone you really love, you could do anything for her even you could give up your life for one whom you love. She is really too lucky to have you."

I kept pleading to my CUTIE o come up till Saturday morning, the day to depart for the tour.

It was Saturday and bus was scheduled to depart at 5:00 am. Last night when we had a talk with my CUTIE, I told her that I didn't have any of her photographs and asked her to please give her photo by coming up on the terrace when I was to depart for the school and she was able to easily hand over her photo to me.

Early in the morning it was around 4:15 am, I departed from my home with one of my friend Sahil for the school. I called her to tell her that I would be there in a few minutes. I was too happy to know that she was early awake and was eagerly waiting for my call. Anyway we reached near to home with a camera in my hand. It was still damn too dark, but all thanks to the street light.

As soon as reached near to her house I could see her standing on the terrace and just waiting for me. I was so happy to see her and then I adjusted my position to have a nice click of her, and yeah I did, I took her photo and just stopped for a moment to see her for some more time, I was lost, when my friend reminded me that we are going to be too late. Then I bid her goodbye waving my hand and heading towards to the school with my friend.

We were there at the school, the corridor was filled with the noise of discussion and the excitement among the students, we all of our classmates were together and were too excited to depart as soon. Then after a moment the announcement was made and we all were asked to move into the bus.

The bus departed and we all were on the drive, a long drive… In our bus most of the students were our classmates. Everyone was busy in singing, dancing, laughing aloud, teasing around; all were surrounded with the classmates except me! I was all alone without my CUTIE with a photo of her in my camera and continuously editing it inorder to make it more beautiful.

Every time I thought about her, the memory of the past rode away in my mind and I could feel her virtual presence there with me. Whenever it happened that she was with me anywhere I thought as if I had the whole world with me but today everyone was with me except her and I felt so lonely there.

Somewhere down the drive my eyes were wet thinking about her and not being with her. My condition was clearly understandable by my all friends both girls and boys. Later on they made me sit right infront of the seat from where I could be involved in every activity. I didn't want to indulge myself in those games yet I had to do so.

We reached on the destination and roam to the places and we did shopping too. I had bought too many things for my mother, sister, brother and ofcourse for my CUTIE too. I also bought a statue of Lord Buddha and a wrist watch that looked completely awesome and cute, that was truly made for my CUTIE. We had everything like lunch, snacks, entertainment and visiting to the places of interest and historical advantages. We reached back home late at night.

On Monday we all reached school and I too with a gift I had taken for her. I gave that to my CUTIE and yes she accepted it with much love. She was there early at the school as I rang up to her and urged her to come early so that I may give her the gift and also we too may get some time. We both explained to each other that how much did we miss, and had a long talk with her.

One day when we had a talk in the evening she told me that her cousin sister was getting married and she wished that

I may come at the marriage. I hesitated a little, but how could I resist myself when my CUTIE was calling me. I agreed to come at the venue; it wasn't far from my house where the marriage was going to be attended.

I told my mom that two days from then I had to attend the marriage ceremony of my friend's sister, and I asked her to purchase a gift which I could give it to them. My mother bought the gift next day itself, and I didn't know what that was as it was already packed and wrapped. I didn't try to open and see it as I knew that the choice of my mom was perfect, it would perfectly make them happy after they see the gift.

At the day of the marriage she called me in the evening to ask the time I was about to reach there. She wished that I would come soon. It was winter so the sun too ran away early from the sky and left behind the black cover of darkness. So I thought to go early and return back in time. I was there before 8:00 pm.

I tried to scan her with my eyes but I always met with the failure, I was very much eager to see her and I couldn't stop myself so I rang to her and informed her about my presence. She came out in the open where the grooms along with the 'Barat' were to sit as I was already sitting there. Though we couldn't talk like we did in the school but all of the best thing was that we could see each other and could share our feelings through emotions!!!!!

We both smiled seeing each other. We talked on the phone rather than talking directly face to face, it seemed that I was having a video call with her. She looked stunning in her green and pink 'Lehenga'. We talked on phone facing each other with the eye contact for sometime and then she went inside again.

I took the chair, turned it around and faced the side from where she would come. Whenever she would get a chance to come back she did and again we had some exchange of the emotions. I was happy as I could see her for more time in a day. This was quite nice day even, I just faced that side waiting for her to come and as she came I just stood up to make her realize that I was still there waiting for her.

I had the gift to be given to bride's mother so when she came again I asked her to show me the bride's mother so that I could hand over the present to her.

She let me knew by signaling her eyes, pointing to the particular direction. I went closer to that lady and congratulated her by handing her the gift. I was a little afraid that what if she asked me that who I was? Or whose son was I then what would I do? But nothing such happened, I felt quite relieved and took a long breathe.

She took it generously and asked me why I was alone and where were my parents. By her words I understood that she was not to be worried about and she didn't recognize as an outsider and may be considering me as a known person, well that didn't concern to any of my business all it mattered that I was safe and could have my CUTIE infront of me every time.

"No aunty! Mom's health isn't good and father is out of the city. So, I had to come myself".

That what was I told her as the answer for her question. She didn't notice me anymore and went to attend some other guests waiting for her.

I ranged back to my CUTIE to inform her that I was returning back to the home as my mom continually kept on calling me as it had gone too late and she was waiting for me at home. O'er that CUTIE asked me whether I had dinner or not, and in case I didn't then all of the first I needed to have it and then to think about leaving.

She trapped me so I too kept forward a condition before her that I would dine only if she was there with me to have it together. Now I trapped her, and she too didn't refuse and boldly agreed to go for that, although it was too difficult but she came to give me the company. We both took the plate and went in the line going parallel to the stall. We were crawling towards the stall and at the same time we had a little talk.

I appreciated about her dress and her stunning look. She was happy to know that and also felt shy. I loved her reaction and asked her not to shy there in crowd. Both of us took very less in terms of the quantity as I was in a hurry to reach home soon but at the same time I wanted to spend some more time standing beside my CUTIE and having a soft talk. I wished God to slow down the time for me and let me stay there for some more time so that I may have some more pics of my CUTIE captured in my mind. But how could He do so, it was not only for me as He needs to cover for the whole world, so my wish was discarded by Him.

She took little food because she wasn't willing to have at that time but it was only for me that she had the dinner. We finished what we had taken in our plate and just a while after I looked at her for the last time that night.

I could easily find a hidden sadness behind her smiling face that was due to my departure, yet she was much happy as I was there at that night to spend some time with her. I waved her goodbye and left for the home reminding her to take care of herself and I went onn.

It was October and few days later a very famous festival in India, in which the wives of married couples used to fast for the whole day without seeking a drop of water for the long live of their husband, and this festival is called "Karva-Chauth" and it was going to be held.

I didn't know much about it except for the fasting done by the wives for the whole day. My CUTIE ranged up to me and talked to me about the festival and wished to keep fast for me. I strictly refused her, disallowing the permission to do so, but she was a 'real stubborn', she overrode my permission and was determined to do it. I didn't have any problem with the festival all I wanted that my CUTIE shouldn't be troubled due to it, as the fast is kept for the whole day and I was afraid that if something went wrong to her health due to the fast. She kept on asking me for the permission and finally she convinced me, I had to drop down my orders inorder to make her happy.

Then I too decided to go for the fast, I thought that if Tamannah could do it for me then why can't I, so I too made my mind not eat or drink until she broke her fast. I kept it as a secret within me, as if she knew that I too was fasting then she would surely make me to not to do that. I know she loves me a lot but I love her more than she loves me, so I too made my mind to fast.

Now it was the day of 'Karva-Chauth'. I made silly reasons before my mom for not having the breakfast and not to carry any lunch box with me while going to school, but my mom kept it in my bag without my knowledge. I took the oath not to have a single bit to eat or drink. In the school I asked her about the fasting and she shook her head giving a positive response. She asked me to come nearby her house in the evening when the moon would be sighted.

"Is it necessary to come near to your house?" I said in a teasing manner.

"No, absolutely not. Don't come. Nothing will happen; I will only break the fast next day when I will see you." She showed her sweet anger.

"You getting naughtier;"

"You too, naughty."

"Ok! Fine, I will reach to your house but for that I need to know the time for the arrival."

"Don't worry as soon as I see the moon I will make you a call and then you come!!! Till then I would do all the necessary rituals."

"Ok! Madam Ji!!"

During lunch break I handed my lunch to my friends to finish it, otherwise I would be scolded at home by home minister. My friends were always ready to finish as much number of lunch boxes they would get. It was less than a minute that I have handed them my lunch and it was completely finished. My friends were too talented at this work. It was the very first time that I was benefited by their extraordinary talent. I was proud of my friends. God Bless them with more such lunch boxes.

During class I went out to wash my face. I went and washed the face and during the act I took a handful of water and put it in my mouth and swallowed it, as if I was not in my own conscious. I didn't even thought about the fast. When I entered the class my eyes went straight onto Tamannah and then I finally realized what actually I did. I cursed myself for that sin. I kept on asking God, why he coaxed me. It was all without my will. It happened without any intention and out of innocence. I knew God will forgive me as well as my CUTIE, but I knew propensity was my habit.

I kept on abusing and cursing myself. I was a sinner at that time, every time when I would see her face, it made me realize that what I had done and then I abused myself more than before. I kept on thinking that what made me to do so, why did I drink the water. The process continued till that evening arrived. However I didn't eat or drink anymore from then and paid more attention in not doing so.

In the evening rain was drizzling and so it wasn't so clear to spot the moon. It was far more time as expected for the moon to show its face. I was feeling hungry but not anything before my CUTIE broke the fast. I kept telling the moon to show its shine and to freed my CUTIE from the fast and let her please, have some food as she too, might be much hungry, so I prayed to rise soon. I wasn't bothered for myself but it was all for my CUTIE. I kept praying and thinking for her that the moon may rise soon and then she would be alright.

Here my phone rang and it was CUTIE on the other side, she showed her joy and said that she had seen the moon, and then she urged me to come to her place. I started from my house by walk without opting to take my bicycle. The rain had made the way too muddy so it was quite uneasy to walk through it and I had to drive my more attention on that. As soon as I was about to reach I called her to inform her that I would be there soon and she replied me that she was already waiting for me on the terrace.

In no moment, I was there and found her on the roof as she said. I stopped myself there. When she saw me, she too asked me to stay still for a while and then she did some 'puja' by looking at me and then broke her fast with the water infront of me. Then she signalled me to leave as her parents were there on the roof and if they find me then, everything was going to be bad so I decided to move on and gave her the flying kiss and biding her Good Night and then I left to my place and broke the fast by taking water.

Next day in school she called me and gave me the lunchbox completely filled with sweets and home made snacks. She strictly ordered me to have it alone and not to give it to anyone else. O'er that I asked her the reason for that, she replied that the sweets were only to be eaten by the husband after the 'puja' has been completed.

"But we aren't married and I am not your husband!!", I asked her in curiosity, I just wanted to hear that she wanted me to be her husband.

"It little differs in my case. These 'prashads' are mend for the expected future husband. Getting my point."

"Yes Madam.", I was full of joy from inside but I didn't tried to show it, I just smiled and replied her back but internally I was in heaven.

She gave me the lunch and asked me to return it the next day as she knew that I couldn't finish that much of sweets at a time in the school as it was so much for me. I kept the lunch inside my bag and took out the present which I brought for her to give on 'Karva-Chauth'. I presented it before her and she felt so happy by getting that, she immediately kept that into her bag so that no one could see it.

It was time for our final exam. We accelerated our studies to get high marks and a respectful position in the class. We studied hard, days and nights, everything was devoted to the studies. During those days we had talks at night too when everyone was asleep and we studied.

Days were getting closer and closer for our exams. She was also good at studies, I knew. I was just trying every sort of things inorder to achieve higher marks.

It was day for our final exam and all of us were busy in last minute revision. We all wished good luck to each other. I went close to my CUTIE stayed there looking at her and then wished good luck for exam. Luckily according to the seating arrangement for the exam my CUTIE was to sit in the room where I was going to give the exam. She was some what six to seven benches behind me in the same row.

As I entered into the room I rolled my eyes into the whole class just to feel the exam, then I scanned the class searching for my CUTIE and yeah I found her, I was happy that the fate was with me. She was already looking at me, I saw her and gave a smile to show her that I was much happy to see her there in my class, she too replied with a sweet smile.

Teacher then entered into the class with answer sheets and the question papers in hand. We were given the material and then got busy in writing the answers. Exams went good for us, we had the sufficient time between the consecutive papers so that we could have good revision. Days passed and so our exams, all the exams went good and now it was the time for our vacation of about fifteen days.

During the vacation we did talk a little more than before whenever we had times we hanged up with each other. After few days our results were declared and all of us were promoted to the next class.

The school gets opened on the scheduled date and we all meet with each other after a long time and share our experience about the vacation. I and my CUTIE as usually reached early in the school so that we may have a long talk without anyone's intervention and also to spend some time with her as I didn't even meet her a once however I tried a lot yet failed. Now we were in the school too early, but there were the persons who couldn't bear our good days and became hurdle, it was our principal and his partner.

Some of the workers who saw us once and kept noticing for our early arrival to the school informed the principal for this deed. Although the principal didn't say anything directly to us but his announcement regarding arrival of school was directly pointed towards us, so he said not to come to school early. I knew that till then hardly anyone was there who wasn't aware about our relation and so the principal, but the fact was that we never got caught red handed in the school, so no one did think of curbing our love. We were tensed that, how could we get time for each other, then I said to her not to arrive early to the school for a week or two and then again we would continue with our same routine.

It was the last week of March and my birthday was not far enough, it was to arrive in April. I decided to do something new this birthday with Tamannah. I thought to take her away somewhere, where we could spend some time together and may have no fear of getting caught as we were frightened then to meet together in early morning in the college. But when I disclosed my idea to my CUTIE then she shook her head and showed her negligence to come. She further clarifies that her parent would never allow her to go anywhere alone. I became disappointed as she wouldn't be there with me on my birthday. Then she gave me the consent that she would surely go with me some other day but not on the day of my birthday. I asked her the reason then she replied that her parents go to Delhi in every two to three months for regular check-up, during that time she would come with me. She added that her parents were going on 7th April so she could come after that. This made me quite happy and I was very excited and was eagerly waiting for the day to come.

Actually her mother is a cancer patient and so visit Delhi every two to three months for the regular check-up in AIIMS as per the appointment given by the doctor.

Anyway she agreed to come on 8th of April. I surveyed a lot for the best restraunt for both of us. I visited several restraunts and also asked from many of my friends.

My birthday arrived and again the same wishes, the same people and I at last my wallet spared empty. The extraordinary thing at this time on my birthday was that, my CUTIE was there with me and she too had given me the birthday present. The person who rejected my treat last year was enjoying it with me. Who didn't even talked a single time nor wished me previously was there standing by my side.

I was too eager to unpack the gift given by her, my friends too were waiting madly and always poked me to unpack the gift given by her. They sometimes snatched the gift and threatened me to open it at once but I refused them. After that they got completely mad and were going to open it on their own, I was afraid if something went wrong. However I got it back after sometime by losing my energy and by making them understood. But they were really out of their brain and again after sometime they repeated their act. This time it took me longer than before to convince them. I had to promise them to show it the next day.

I went home and calmly sat in my room and kept the gifts aside as my parents were at home so I thought not to open at that time. But I couldn't stop myself and just went into the room and unpacked my CUTIE's gift slowly. I could see the perfume packed in the wooden box having a glass in the upper portion. I opened the box with much love and care, took out that perfume and applied a little on my body, its fragrance was out of the world. I took that perfume in my hand and kept on looking at it. After a while my mumma came near to my room calling out my name and searching for the source of fragrance, I was unaware of my mom's arrival and was busy in looking at that perfume.

My mom stood still at the gate and she started looking at me to find out what was I trying to find out in that bottle. She made me awake by calling out my names standing there at the door and then I was back into my conscious and was shocked to see my mom there.

It was 8th of April and the day of our first ever date. But this time she couldn't come with an ease as it was expected, her grand- parents interrupted the plan as they didn't allow her to go out. So she decided to come in her school uniform so that her parents may thought that she had left for the school. A day before it, I had showed her the way by which she could reach the main road and wait for my arrival.

I dressed up casually and when my mom asked the reason for that, I replied that I was going for the science exhibition instead of going to the school along with my friend. I knew that my mom would do anything to send me to the world of science so I gave her the mind cherishing answer, she was happy to let me go for their.

I dressed up quickly and sat just near to the phone waiting for her call. It was long that I have been waiting for the call and it made me tensed but I had complete trust on my CUTIE. And then after a little while the phone rang, it was she, and gave me the missed call inorder to signal me to leave from the house for her.

I left the house and quickly ran towards to the place where we had planned to meet. I hurried up yet I found myself slow so I opted to run and reach there quickly as I couldn't allow my CUTIE to wait much. As I reached on the loop road I saw her heading towards the main road, she was around twenty feets ahead of me, I too moved closer to her. She searched me all around and then she turned back and found me, giving a sweet smile of satisfaction to have me there. I went too close to her and asked her to wait beside the main road till I bring a taxi or any other vehicle to go. Then I signaled her and she arrived quickly and sat on the vehicle beside me.

We were towards our destination. Ten minutes later we were there at the restraunt. We got inside and sat on the same side, along with each other. It was the place where we had to spend some time of around three to four hours.

I asked her to sit infront of me facing towards me, earlier she refused then she agreed. Now we could easily have an eye contact with each other, our hands were interlocked in each others hand and there was a wave of love that flowed through us. We kept watching each other and a current ran into me, that was the soothing effect of love.

We then ordered some snacks and drinks for both of us. She quickly came beside me then, as she was feeling uneasy there. We talked more with our eyes than our mouth, our lips were jealous of the eyes as they hardly received the chance to move and utter a word.

It was my first time that I was out with someone so close and was spending time for a long time. While talking with our eyes we moved closer to each other, however it wasn't my intention, but something attracted me to go near to her and then suddenly something did go wrong and we started kissing each other, it was for a while and then we were apart. This time she wasn't shying and her eyes were glittering more than before. I took a turn to talk then. We talked a lot, we kept silent a lot, and also we loved a lot. We had to spend time together by keeping a thought in my mind that she had to reach her house before 2 o'clock and for that I had to be very responsible and punctual in the terms of promise made to her to drop her home in time.

We were sitting next to each other such that our body was in contact and our hands were interlocked with other. Although we didn't go out to move through the places yet we had much fun there.

It was time for us to left for our homes. I kissed on her fore head before we left. I paid the bill and then left for the home. We took an auto to go back to home. It was noon time and the road was filled with the traffic, there was much rush than ever before on the road and it was going to be a hurdle to reach home in time. She held my hands and saw me, I too saw her and could easily find nervousness and also she was a bit afraid, I asked her to remain calm and tried to convince her that we would be on time. Yet she was restless and disagreed me by giving the reason to the traffic and the speed of the auto.

I kept my hands around her shoulder and hugged her. I then ordered the driver to fasten the speed of his auto. It was too much rush on the road and the driver too didn't want to take any risk of driving fast. I said myself that if the condition goes like that then surely we would be late and this would make my CUTIE more frightened. I then talked to the auto driver to drive fast and if he made us reach before time then I would pay double the fare.

Listening to this he tried to do everything he could. Now I could see him doing something for us. He worked out a lot to find new ways and made us reach there in time. I paid him as I promised and we started moving on foot towards her home. Now she was much relaxed and felt safe as she knew that she would reach home before time.

She reached her home ten minutes earlier than the expected time. I bid her goodbye and I left for the home. We both turned around at the same time and gave smile to each other.

I was on the way to my home and I danced a lot throughout the way as if the instrumentals were being played around me everytime. As soon as I reached home all of the first I did, to call her and asked her whether anyone knew about us or not. She was calm and happy, which reflected that everything was right and she too was very happy for the day as it went on successfully.

Our decision to bunk the school that day was known to everyone in the class and all were waiting for the next day to arrive so that they may tease and asked me the whole story.

We reached the school the next day and everyone was on me, all eyes were on me no matter boys or girls. All smiled and gathered around me keeping me as the nodal centre. They all had a same question with them that how was my date and what special, if happened. They kept on forcing me and provoking me to answer to their question but I kept numb. Anyhow I got a narrow escape.

One day she made me came across a very interesting thing which I didn't even noticed till then. She told me that, she was a very big devotee of "Hanumanji" and for that she did fast on every Tuesday and every sort of good things that had happened to her was on the day of Tuesday. She also let me knew that the day when I proposed her was Tuesday, the day we kissed each other for the first time was Tuesday, and the day of our first ever date was also Tuesday. I was really very surprised to know that and was happy too by knowing that God is with us and surely our fate would shine.

If all the incidents happened in my life were pre-planned then there would be no matter of the surprise but these things happened accidentally with us. I never planned to propose her that day as I wasn't mentally prepared, rather it was due to some of mine and hers good friends who forced me to propose at that particular day.

The kiss too was accidental and now the date too happened on Tuesday it was just because of her parents, rather being planned.

She also made me know that both days when I kissed her was Tuesday and eventually I broke her fast. However the events might have broken her fast but yet she wasn't ever angry or guilty o'er that, as she left everything on "Hanuman-ji", that anything he would do would be good to her in anyway.

I was too pleased and impressed to listen that, how deeply she was in love and observed every incident minutely and also she was ready everytime to sacrifice everything for me. I felt much proud and found myself too lucky to have her with me.

I always used to have candy everyday while going to the school. That day I ate a candy and still I had one left with me lying in pocket. I reached school and then got busy in talking to my CUTIE. I slide my hand inside my pocket while talking to her, I didn't understood that, what was that, so I took it out to see that was still left in my pocket. It was my favorite candy. I gave it to my CUTIE and from then onwards it became my daily routine to give one candy to my CUTIE everyday.

I don't know whether, did she like it or not? but it was my perception that everyone would love to have that candy so sweet and sour. Some of my classmates usually tease me about what had I done to her or what else had happened at the date so that she gets a candy everyday and that too, one very sour and sweet 'kaccha mango bite'.

After some days our summer vacations were to start and I was unhappy as we would not meet each other the whole vacation.

Vacation started and so we only had talk everyday via phone. While going to the coaching I always opted the route that took me to her house and there I would then threw two candies on her roof everyday without her knowledge. I did the same the whole vacation.

A long way and then the vacation ended and the school re-opened and then again we started going to the school.

That day I decided to ask Tamannah about what Yash had told me long time before. When I told her what Yash had told me then she smiled and said that Yash was right what he saw but was wrong at what he heard.

I didn't understood her words. She smiled again and further added that it was true that, she was giving a gift to a boy but he was Mantasha's boy friend and it was his birthday that's why she called him near to the school but felt shy to go near to him to give the gift as all the students would have seen her doing so. So she gave her the gift to handle it to her boy-friend. So she gave the gift to him and that very moment itself

Yash would have seen her and might have interpreted wrong regarding her.

I was already confirmed and had full belief on her and yeah I was proved right.

On the day when school re-opened, it was the half day class in school and it was the sudden announcement to close the school at the half day by saying that no more classes would go on after the lunch.

I thought that it would be a great day and we could get some time to spend together.

I asked Tamannah and gave her the idea that, we may go at any restraunt after the dismissal from the school and could stay together for some time, but she was afraid. She was worried that her parents would know about it.

I asked her not to worry and our parents were unaware of the half day and we had much time to spend and also they would never come to know about us. She still feared that, she wouldn't reach home in time but I assured her and promised her to leave her home safely on time, o'er this she agreed to go with me.

We were waiting for the dismissal and I was too eager for that. As soon as the dismissal bell rang we together hurried up and moved towards the restraunt. We were there within half an hour.

It was the same restraunt and we opted the same place to sit together. This time she flawlessly sat infront of me without any fear and took my hand in her hand, I was aroused more than shocked and happy too that she took a chance t do that, I was feeling so lucky to have that kind of girl with me, she always made me feel great.

It was nice sitting there, looking at her and no one to disturb or distract us. Sitting along-with Tamannah there with our hands interlocked made me feel like I was staying in heaven with the most beautiful girl in the world that God had ever created. I just wanted to stay there and keep looking at her continuously and just begging the time to slow down its speed and let me have my CUTIE stayed infront of me forever.

We stayed there, talked about us, about our families and many more. We stayed there more than two hours and had much talks and fun and also had some snacks, and then we left the place.

We came back to our home at the desired time so that no one could know about our plan and might not suspect us. I dropped her near to her house and left for my home, and when I reached my home I called her immediately that, if everything was alright or not? She was positive and this made me relaxed. She was happy to spend time with me and so was I. I was too happy to have her.

Days were passing too quickly. Everyday we talked in the school and on the phone too. Whole day in the school we stole the glimpse of each other either by hook or by crook. After dismissal from the school I went to the coaching directly from there. As I entered the coaching the junior girls passed the smile to me. She came closer and whispered in ears that she had something very important to tell me. I asked to tell quickly and immediately.

I was eager to know as I thought that she was going to reveal something new about my CUTIE. She shams of shyness. We were being starred by each student in the coaching at that very moment. I was the senior most and she was a class junior to me, but she stood so close as if she was my girlfriend. I took a step away from her and then ordered her to say, what she wanted or else she may go away from there.

What she said at that time was hard to be believed and quite unexpected for me and my ears and might be for anyone else too. She said that, 'Sadaf', her best friend, and 'Smita', younger sister of my classmate, wanted a kiss from me. She was crazy for me and always looked for me in the school. First-of-all, 'Sadaf' wanted that, I should be her boyfriend and if not, then at-least a kiss to her. Everyone present over there looked paused and were eyeing on me after listening to her words.

My face was redder than a tomato with anger. I scolded her for behaving like that and said, "It wasn't anything to tell to your senior with a smile on your face. You should be ashamed of yourself uttering such words." And then further I ordered her to make her friend understood quite well that I really didn't have any feeling for her and everyone in the school knew about my love story and storey going on smoothly with my CUTIE. I was and I would be honest and loyal to my CUTIE and I didn't even thought to cheat her.

Firstly I thought to inform that deed to her elder sister who was my classmate at the time and a very good friend of mine, but I realized that it may lead to the misunderstandings between the sisters and I didn't want to spoil the relationship between them, so I kept it with me and further thought that she would automatically understood if I wouldn't pay attention to her. This scene was very unexpected for me and continuously I thought that how could it be so, that a girl would directly come to me and ask for a kiss without even knowing me completely!!

I was really shocked but I didn't lose my senses and responded her positively, which was appreciable for me!!!

We were in 10th standard and this time we had to give our board examinations. Everyone was aiming to achieve higher marks and so they seemed to be serious regarding their studies and so were busy with the books always. Our school and love life was going together hand in hand.

It was the month of August and the preparation for the Independence Day was on the high speed. Daily practice of the marching was done in the school campus and other programmes were revised under our supervision.

All the students in the school were divided into the four houses, blue, green, red, and yellow named after the four legends of Indian history and they were, Gandhi-ji, Nehru-ji, Sardar patel and B.R.Ambedkar. I was in the yellow house. Marching was done according to the houses, each house had its one leader and he was the person who led the whole house as a team, there was one head who lead the whole school and he was the school captain. Each house along with its captain, had a vice captain too. When we had the marching practice, I oftenly left my house and went into the blue house because my CUTIE belonged to the blue house and I went beside her.

I went there and commanded them to learn and made them to practice well, all were aware with my actual work and so they teased me by saying that, my yellow house would sink if I continued to go to the other houses and made them practice, leaving my house in a mess.

Sahil was the blue house captain so he never objected me, rather he did laugh at me by my activity. My house captain too was the good friend of mine so he just pleaded me not to go but I was not in a state to listen to anyone and I just went to her in her house just to be with her.

During those times I instructed less and talked more to my CUTIE. CUTIE and Mantasha were always together as they both were in the same house. We always talked and others were always ready to tease me. It didn't matter at all for me as, I was happy with my CUTIE.

One day it rained quite heavily at the night, whole night the rain continued with full of its strength and just stopped for a while to take a breathe and then again continued, there wasn't any sign that the rain would stop completely.

The sky showed its full angriness by the repeated and the regular thundering sound during the rain. Rain continued till the morning and it was the time for us to left for school. I knew somehow that the school would remain close due to these conditions even if we went there. So rather going directly to the school I made a phone call and tried to know the exact condition, but the weather condition didn't allow me to make any phone call.

Somehow I got connected to one of the person from the school management and then I continued.

"Hello!", it was the staff on the other side.

"Good Morning Sir!".

"Good Morning".

"Sir, I wished to know that will the school be remain open today?"

"No, the school will remain closed for the day as it had been raining heavily since night".

"Thank You Sir!"

"You are welcome, and please inform it to your friends too."

"Ok Sir."

"Good bye!"

I disconnected the phone and it was exactly what I thought. I already knew this in these ten to twelve years of schooling, as two-three such conditions have occurred, that the school was closed due to the heavy rainfall.

I thought to inform Tamannah too as she might be worried, so I ranged up to her, she picked the call and I asked her whether she did called to school or not and then I informed her everything regarding the closing of the school for the day. We had a little talk as her parents were there with her so we disconnected the call soon.

After half an hour the rain stopped and the sky was so clear that no one could find even a sign of the cloud which might rain. No more rain that day and if it would occur then not at that time but after some hour. The weather, too cool and pleasant, it was too romantic.

Everyone would love to spend time with their loved one and so was with me. I also wanted to spend some time with my CUTIE, but how? It was holiday in the school. How would she bunk? How could we meet? These thoughts were running in my mind. I knew one thing about her family that, they had blind faith on CUTIE. Whatever she would say to her parents they would agree and trust her blindly.

I called her back to tell my plan. She was also ready to meet and spend that day with me, but was little nervous and afraid for the reason to be caught telling lie. I gave her the idea to tell her parents that the school was closed for all others, but being the senior most and also for the preparation for our board exams, school was opened only for 10th standard for some extra classes in science and maths. She agreed to tell what I told her.

It was still drizzling outside, she said everything as I told her and she was granted with permission to go. She again called me to inform and give the good news, I told her the location along-with the time so that we could meet there and then move to some other place.

I dressed up and waited for her call. She called me soon when she was about to leave. I hung up the call and hurried myself to reach to the pre-planned place. I reached there before her arrival and waited a little for her when I saw a beautiful girl wind-up in the sky-colored dress holding an umbrella in one hand and heading towards me, it was none other than my CUTIE.

I still remember her smile at that time when she saw me waiting for her. I was really in love with her smile and in love with everything she does, it looks so cute. It was the very first time when I had seen her in the casual dress. She looked like any angel from the fairy world of the fairy tale. I lost my consciousness and kept looking at her.

She came to me by crossing the road to other side and we bid hello to each other and then we sat in the auto. I wanted to go somewhere else other than the restraunt to spend so much pleasing day, but there was always a chance of rain which would shower anytime. So, unwantedly I had to opt for the restraunt.

We reached there and paid the fare. We straight away went towards the restraunt and found that it had not yet opened. Not only the restraunt but also the shops were closed and wasn't open at the time we reached. Hardly any shops were opened.

It was around 10 o' clock and I remembered that upto then whole market was filled with the crowd, it was just because of the rain that didn't allow many people to move out of their houses.

I looked everywhere to find any shop or place where we could stay. I then found a clinic which was opened; I went there and asked Tamannah to sit there, while I went for searching the better place. She agreed me and I walked out to search, I went through many places but didn't get much.

I then thought to return back to my CUTIE as she might be waiting for me. While I was returning back to my CUTIE, I found the same restraunt opened where we had our first date. Now I need not to bother a lot as got the best option available to spend time.

I reached happily to my CUTIE and asked her to come with me. We went out and she followed me, and reached to the restraunt and became the first ever customer of the day.

Wherever we go our hands were always interlocked. We talked about ourselves and about the pleasant weather that forced me to meet her that day itself and made the moment romantic.

Usually people make the day romantic with some special treatment given by them to their partner and some days itself are romantic as made by the almighty and it was one of them.

We had a lot of talks and we talked and talked and talked. In the restraunt most of the times my hand was around her shoulder and her head was on my shoulder. I wanted that moment to stay for the whole life.

It showed that she had full trust on me and on my love. After two hours we had to leave for the home or else she would be questioned a lot. We went on happily for the reason that we spent that splendid day together. Before we left I kissed on her fore head.

There wasn't so rush and not much vehicles were running on the road as it had rained rained heavily, so we had a smooth drive to home.

I dropped her near to her house. she passed me a sweet and cute smile and went inside her house. I too returned back to my home happily thinking about the every moment that occurred and just smiled to have such a pleasant and the loving moment with her.

At night I was having my dinner and at the same time she called me up. I immediately put aside my dinner and ran to wash my hands to pick up her call quickly. I picked her call and on the other side she seemed to be much afraid, and she was about to weep. I asked her whether everything was alright?

"No, Dad knew it, that I had lied them." She replied in a vibrating voice which showed her fear.

"How could they know?"

"Because of the tuition teacher."

"Tuition teacher!! But how?", I asked her.

She was being taught by the school teacher itself at home, but I couldn't understand that, how could it lead to such problem?

"Sir had given me homework but I couldn't completed it, o'er that he asked me the reason for that and asked me that, what did I do the whole day as the school was also closed? At that very moment my grandmother arrived into the room and heard everything and added that I had gone for the extra classes and that's how all the things had happened." CUTIE further explained.

"What was the reaction of your parents and especially of your father?" I enquired.

"My father didn't say a single word to me and nor is he speaking to me from that moment. And from now my school is forbidden as per ordered by my father to my mom.

"What?" I was shocked to know this.

"Yes darling!"

"How could I live without you?"

"Why will you live without me? I will always be with you." She tried to make me calm down as I got disturbed.

"If you would not come, how would my days pass?" I was worried a lot.

"Please don't think, that I am away, just think I am with you."

"Ok! But how can I live without seeing you?" I was still worried.

"Same here darling! May be for some days my father wouldn't allow me to come."

"No, you have to come for me." Now I started acting like a child, that I only wanted her.

"Please darling. I couldn't do anything. I too am tensed and helpless." Now she too expresses her problem.

She further clarifies, "May be I can't talk to you for much time for some days."

"Ok. But you have to talk everyday." I urged her.

"Ok. I will try." She replied trying to convince me and make me calm down.

We hanged-off the phone with our eyes wet. She was really too tensed and afraid as it was very clear from her voice, still she cared for me, she didn't want that I would be worried a lot so she always tried to calm me down by over-hiding her real condition. But she couldn't hide that from me. I knew everything and so I too was tensed a lot and couldn't eat that night nor did I sleep the whole night.

I just kept thinking about her with tears in my eyes lying on the bed and thinking about her condition. I was so helpless at the first time, as I couldn't interfere much in this matter or it would lead to the huge problem.

Next day in the school everybody could see me sad, fighting for the happiness. My happiness was my CUTIE. Everyone understood that something really bad had happened with me. My eyes were red as I didn't sleep the whole night.

Whenever anyone asked me about that, my eyes went wet. Anyhow I told everything to my friends after they insisted. When I completed the narration I was left with tears in my eyes and cheeks and I was crying infront of my friends, infront of the girls and infront of the whole class. My smile had vanished. Almost every girl and my friends tried a lot to take me out of the grief and take me back to the happiness but they all were unsuccessful. I was numb and kept thinking about her and could only weep.

Girls always told me to get out of the grief and to be as I was. They too said that, smile on my face suited better than the sadness. But I couldn't be happy as there was no reason to be happy. No one could understand the height of my grief.

I was just quite the whole day in the school and didn't talk to anyone neither in the school nor at home.

My condition was more pathetic for others. How could they tolerate me sitting so numb, as I had been always known for my mischief and notorious acts. I used to smile everytime and let others do the same.

Many times I thought that apart from living such life its better to end up, but yet there was a slight ray of hope that some day she would surely come up and hug me and would take me back to the original form prohibited me from committing any scene.

There was no one to see me, no one to care for me, no one who would slide her hands on my hairs, no one who would rest her head on my shoulder and no one's shoulder on whom I could keep my hand and find someone so close to me. Everything was lost, I had a vast grief inside which oftenly splashes out in the form of tears from my eyes. I cried and cried only for her.

At that time my best friend was my loneliness, atleast due to which I could recall her in my thoughts and my dreams. Her thought would give me only sadness and tears, but still I wanted myself to keep myself lost in her thought and memories.

As much more time I spent in her thought more and more tears sprinkled from my years just showering to my cheeks, and I felt myself much closer to her. I needed her very much and was missing her too badly. I couldn't count a single second that I had not spent in thinking of her. I continually cried for her whole day and night.

In the school every girl wanted to have a talk with me to share my pain and requested me everytime to be happy, but instead of talking to them I just ignored them. Nothing seemed good without her, the world felt so lonely without her; I was always in search of the unknown happiness without her.

Her thought rolled into my mind everytime and they made me sad.

Shalini always tried to made me understood everytime whenever she gets the opportunity, but nothing moved me, I stayed numb and ignored them as I just wanted only Tamannah.

It was third consecutive day in the school that she was absent and I too was from my soul. I was physically present but mentally I was not in the world. That day seeing me crying for my CUTIE in the class Shalini came to me along-with some more girls and tried to made me understood.

My friends were all tired up in convincing me but I was a real stubborn and didn't even move an inch from my thought and condition.

When Shalini talked to me I told her that if she really wanted to see me happy then please to go to Tamannah's house and talk to her mother and anyhow convince her to send her back to the school. Shalini and all the girls surrounding me agreed at once and had started working at it.

Next day there was a little time left for the morning assembly. I was so curious as, I would know that was she coming to the school or not? I asked all the girls to go right then. All of them moved to CUTIE's house as it was not too far from the school.

They went for me and I was left there waiting for their returning trip, so that, I could know that what did happen. I kept waiting at the main entrance of the school for them to return. After a while they all could be seen coming back, I was much nervous than before and some what excited to hear the good news. As soon as they arrived I immediately went closer to them and asked them to tell what had happened.

Shalini asked me to follow her to the class, and I did as she asked me. I wanted to know the whole scenario. When we reached the classroom, I asked her the question,

"Did you meet Tamannah?"

"Yes we all met her." Shalini responded in low tone.

"How is she?" I questioned her.

"Good but not the best. She cried as soon as we told her the, reason that you had send us." Shalini said.

She further added, "Actually we didn't talk much because her mother didn't leave her alone with us for much time."

"Did you talk to her mother?"

"Yes, we did. But her mother was telling that it was her father's decision. She would go to school whenever her father allow her.", told Shalini.

Listening to this I cried deep inside within me so that no one could listen or feel it. I knew she would come but when would she come? I also knew that she was only mine and no one could take her away from me, but the duration of parting away was getting quite larger.

"We told her that you constantly kept weeping and your smile was lost and even you didn't talk to anyone." Hena said to me when she felt that I was sad again.

"Why did you tell her? It would add up her sadness." I said in the shocking manner as I didn't want her to be sadder.

"She told us all to look after you and not to let you alone for a single moment in the school and try to make you happy." Said Shalini.

"So, please be happy." She further added.

Knowing the whole scene it seemed as if her mother wanted me to wait more for CUTIE and drop more tears.

It was September and our first anniversary was just a week away, but still there was no sign of her. What if, my anniversary would simply go like a sad day without her? This question always ran through my mind and I become sadder than before for this.

It is everyone's desire to celebrate the anniversary with their partner atleast the first one in a lovely and the romantic way. I continuously thought about the day of our anniversary. Why and how to celebrate without her?

I couldn't even makeup myself happy for a single moment even if I wanted for that, then too. All it was that, I was thinking about that day.

I was completely lost. I forgot to shave. I had a full grown beard. I never used to have oil on my head but those days one could easily wash hands by the oil present on my head. I didn't want to shave, for whom I would have shaved. No one to see me, no one to care for me, no one to appreciate my charmness, for whom I would do that?

These days the single good thing happened to me was her glimpse which I could get while going to the school. Actually I always opted for the path that reached her house to go to the school and then there I would get her standing on the terrace. It was my only chance to see her the whole day. I wasn't more than any dead person, almost broken and lost in myself. As the days passed my sadness goes on increasing.

It was now 4th of the September and the next day would be the teacher's day and so all the preparation was going on in the class and school for its celebration. On that day we wrote a letter and invited all the teacher's to our class and then we asked every teacher to make their sign below it. I got a plan from this, and I too wrote a letter for the students to come the next day on the occasion of teacher's day and asked everyone to sign on that letter and then I gave that letter to my junior who actually lived near to my CUTIE's house and told him to go their and brought her signature. I was thinking that if, she would sign, then her parents would allow her atleast for the teacher's day. He went and came after sometime. I took the letter and started searching her name. There it was, yes, she had signed. This ran a slight smile on my face. It made me a little relieved but my happiness would be only at that time when she would be standing infront of me.

He said, "I met her and gave the reason that you had sent me. She asked me about your well-beingness and further said that she would sign but can't come." Hearing this, it took away my slight smile; I just folded the letter and kept it with me for always. As long as my life would be there, I would always have that letter with me. I always opened the letter just to see her name written by her soft hands and touched it to feel her, it made me feel good but yet lonelier than before.

It was 5th of September and as expected almost everyone reached the school on time. Everyone seemed to be very busy in decorating the class but I kept idol and my eyes were stuck at the gates of the class in a hope that she would still arrive.

Shalini came closer to me with some other girls and sat before me tried to talk and make me remember always that, what CUTIE said. She continuously starred at me but I ignored her and asked them to visit again to her house. I pleaded them to go and please convince her mom to send her atleast for today. They all agreed and quickly and departed for the destination.

I don't know what kind of friends did I had, I was so lucky to have them who could do anything to made me happy. My own friends were trying everytime to made me happy and these girls everytime tried to do anything I asked.

I was really proud and to have such a loyal, faithful, trust-worthy and much caring friends. My eyes were constantly at the path the girls would return. After sometime they returned back. I asked them what had happened. They told that her mother didn't allow her to go with them.

"Did you ask for today only?" I questioned.

"Yes!!" said Palak.

"She cried as we told about your condition." Shalini explained.

"She also made us to promise, to keep you happy." She further added.

"Is she well?" I asked.

"Similar to you!!" said Shalini.

"Her mother told that she kept herself inside her room and didn't speak to anyone." Hena said.

Shalini asked me to hold on as I was about to turn back and depart away from them. I froze where I was and questioned her that, what was her wish then?

"Whatever we all have told you about her, is absolutely true, but there is something still left that you should know!!" said Shalini in a dim voice.

"What else? Please tell that to me. Don't try to hide a single thing from me please!!" I begged them.

"Tamannah is really mad for you. She loves you unconditionally and her love is very true for you. From the day her father prohibited her, she has packed herself in her room and has written your name on the wall of her room. If this is the height of her love then also it can be over looked. She had crossed the limits for loving you and missing you. She is on the verge of extinction. Her own identity is endangered. Everyday she cuts her hand from the knife and she had cut down her upper sleeve of her hand just to write your complete name. We saw your name on her left sleeve. It was so clear and big that anyone could clearly read it from far. No one can ever dare to do so, except the one who is completely mad in love. She is completely mad for you dear and is missing you too badly. She loves you. You both are really made for each other. We haven't seen or listened any love story like those of your's. Hat's Off to you and your love. You are facing hardship today but God is not cruel, he may have planned something much better that would happen because of this and also he would make you both together for ever, and you will be seeing each other very soon. We all will pray for you and your love." Shalini was unable to complete her words clearly. Her eyes were wet and her voice got stuck in her throat. She was crying and crying for us, though not letting anyone know about it, but all of us knew it very well.

Her words made me cry too. I was crying for my CUTIE and also for her condition, as explained by Shalini. The whole day I did nothing else than to cry for my CUTIE.

Her love for me was too valuable and she was priceless for me. I had no other option other than to cry. I just wept and allowed my eyes shower my infinite sadness on my cheeks. I spoke to none. Always there some girls surrounding me to make me understood and tried to make me happy even after knowing that, my happiness lies in CUTIE so I had no reason to be happy.

I and my CUTIE were in a huge grief. We wept everytime. I didn't bother to be noticed while crying. Our principle gave a short motivating speech but I hardly listened to any of his word or gave a bit attention to what he said. I was crying in the corner, tears were sprinkling constantly through my cheeks. Everyone came near to me to talk but I ignored and left the celebration in between and headed towards home.

I reached back to the home and bolted the door from inside and cried as much as I could. My eyes were damn red and swollen. I divorced the lunch, dinner and everything and devoted myself in her thought. I felt better when crying then to talk with anyone. I avoided myself going in public. If I didn't had any hope that she would return then I must have committed suicide, but the love itself lies on the condition of hope and so was I.

I cried and prayed to God to please return back my CUTIE, my happiness, my reason to live, my reason to cherish, my everything!!! My mother was totally unaware with my scene. Whenever she asked me the reason for the closed door I always answered her that, I was studying and didn't want to get disturbed.

Everyone in the school and the coaching, either my classmates or my juniors had the news about the situation of the separation. It was more than a week that I hadn't seen my CUTIE. Her father kept her away from the school and from me too. My happiness had completely vanished in vain.

In the lunch break in school I wished to be all alone at that time, no one to disturb me in missing her, no one to force me to be happy without her and no one to calm me down and to stop loving her.

I put forward every possible excuses to be alone and away from everyone. I went to the corner most part of the ground and opted the corner bench to spend some time there with my loneliness or kept standing myself and trying everytime to find any suitable solution to this problem.

Seeing me alone at the corner 'Nisha', a junior girl came to me and asked me that if she could say something to me at that time. Although I didn't wish to listen to her yet, I permitted her to continue.

"You look so cute. You are so attractive too. Everyone would be so proud to be your girlfriend and so I am." She said with a smile on her face.

"I didn't get you. What are you trying to say?"

She looked around to see if anyone was watching us or not, and then again I asked her to clarify her words.

"I mean to say that, I Love You."

"What? Are you crazy? Are you aware about me?" I screamed out in anger and was about to slap her, then I had control over myself and calmed me down.

"Yes, I Love You even after knowing about you and Tamannah. She had made your life worse than ever. She sucks."

She crossed her limit and made me angry than before.

I just burst out into anger and shouted aloud at her saying, "She is only and only mine and I am made for her. Take your ass away from me."

She might have come to me to take the advantage of our separation. I tried to make her understood but she wasn't ready to listen, so I left her alone there and marched away from there, in the midway I turned around to her and shrieked her to forget me or fuck herself up.

The days of our anniversary was getting closer and I could do nothing rather than to cry for her, and begging God to return her back soon. Everyday I went to school in the hope that maybe her parents might allow her to go to the school. All my days passed without any taste and any fun.

My eyes were always wet since her father had prohibited her to go school. I thought myself to be the most unluckiest person those days. I had my love with me but yet too far from me that I couldn't even see her.

I started for the school, when I was close to her house I didn't see my CUTIE standing there on the terrace for me. Maybe her parents got to know it why she went to terrace daily early morning and maybe they had curtail her freedom. My only hope to see her was snatched away from me too harshly.

I was left like a man without soul but only having a physical appearance. If my condition would exist for long then may be I would no longer be considered as a human being or might be, I wouldn't be alive for long without my CUTIE, my oxygen.

She is the only life-giving happiness. Days were passing and I was also about to pass.

I reached school on time and at the entrance a junior girl who called me 'Bhaiya' stood there and smiled at me. I didn't know why she smiled at me. She came closer to me and said

"Ab to hans bhi lo bhai." – Junior.

"I am fine, but why are you telling me to be happy?" –I.

"Get inside the class and search your reason to smile, yourself." –Junior.

I don't know what she meant. I went into the class and there too, everyone was happy for me. Everyone came to me and told me to smile atleast today. I couldn't make out that why did they all said the same thing to me. I placed my bag on my seat and when I was about to turn I saw the bag at the place which was emptied from the past ten days. It was the bag I recognized. It was my Tamannah's bag.

"Is she here?", I asked very impatiently.

"Yes, she is!!" Kaveri said.

"Where is she now?" I was very much impatient and was much excited too.

"Go and search yourself." Shalini said in a teasing manner.

"Please, Please, Please, tell me."

"Ok-Ok, She is waiting for you just outside the class." –Shalini.

I ran away quickly without a second waiting for anyone and saw her standing with Mantasha and was smiling looking at me. I was feeling as if I have got everything, my happiness was back with me, whole world was dancing around me, even the noise of the students felt like any music rolling into my ears.

I called her in the class. She did as I told. We went to the corner of the class and talked.

"How are you?"

"Fine. And you?"

"Very fine seeing you."

"How did you get the permission?"

"I went to my daddy and asked him to permit me to go to school and also I begged her to forgive me for the deed I did. And further pleaded him until he pardoned me."

"Did he agree?"

"Yeah! And that's why I am here infront of you."

"You don't know how good it is to see you, I can't explain them in words."

"Same to me too."

"Anyway you are looking good in your oily hair." She commented.

"And what about beard??"

"To be very honest, I don't like beard."

"Don't see my hair, its too oily."

"But you look nice in it."

I blushed into laughter.

"Are you forgetting something?" CUTIE asked me.

"No, nothing!!!"

"Do I?" I asked her.

"Maybe. I don't know."

"What?"

"I don't know."

There was a smile on her face and mine too after seeing each other. I was getting back into my life. We talked for some more time and during that I asked her many a time that what I was forgetting, but everytime she answered "I don't know".

The bell rang and we went out happily for the assembly. In the class I discovered the situation by which we could see each other. Whenever I wished to see her I just utter aloud 'Palat' and she turned back to me with a cute smile on her face. This tool had been too good to be used to see her.

In the complete day in the school I almost called her 10-15 times by using that word and everytime she turned back with smile.

During the lunch break when we both went together in the corner of the class she again asked me if I am forgetting something. I then continuously kept on asking her that, what was that, but she denied telling anything to me. I tried to remember a lot but couldn't reach any conclusion. Lunch break finished, but still I kept on thinking that, what I was missing then. I asked the same question to my friends, they just answered "How could I know what are you forgetting!!!"

I reached home thinking the same question and then suddenly a thought got struck into my head. I rushed to the calendar to see the date. Oh! My God. What had I done?

It was 11th of September, the date I approached her, the day of our very first anniversary. How could I forget? Oh God! How would I face her now? Then I understood why she asked me every-time, if I had forgotten something. Two days before I remembered every-thing very well and then today, I don't know what happened to me. Maybe the grief of separation had affected me, or maybe the unexpected happiness of the day made me forgot everything. I picked up phone and called her instantly.

I had tried a number of times but she didn't answered to any of my call. Lastly when she picked up, she hurried in saying that her mother was around so she couldn't talk. I started telling her about what had I forgotten. I tried to wish but the phone got disconnected in the mid way. I called her again and again but she didn't answered any of my call.

I rushed towards the cycle and moved to her place in the dress in which I was at home. On the way I called her again and again but nothing happened. I stopped my cycle at the home of a junior and told him to go to her place and ask her to come on her terrace.

He went and did exactly as I told him. He came back running just to inform me that she would be on the terrace anytime.

I rushed to her place and waited outside the gate for her to come on the terrace. I was waiting for her underneath a tree which was just infront of her house. After a moment I saw her, yes, I saw her. She was about to come on the terrace but suddenly she turned around and returned back downstairs as her mom had seen me standing there and so she resisted her to go upstairs. I waited there for a long time in a hope that, she would try to come and I would wish her.

It was too long that I waited then I realised that her mother wouldn't allow her up. I took my step back to home with my heart drowning.

As soon as I reached home I called her again but no response from the other end. Whenever I got time I called her but either her mother or her brother received the call and I had to disconnect it quickly. In that single day I called her more than 100 times but didn't get a response from her. I tried at night even but no fruitful result.

When we didn't get in touch the whole day and the night then I thought that the next day when I reach school I would ask her to forgive me and then I would gift her a present. Though I didn't get any chance to buy any present for her for the occasion so I thought to give it next day.

I reached the school on time and waited for her arrival. My eyes were eagerly waiting to see her. The bell rang but she didn't arrived. I then understood the reason for her absence.

I guessed, her parents didn't allow her to come just because of the reason that I had ranged her many times. I was fed up with the decisions of her parents. This situation was hard to be lived. A day of happiness and then sorrow, I was depressed. She arrived for a day, enlightened the hope to live within me and then left me back to my previous condition. Slowly and steadily I was forced to die. Many times atrocities were committed on me. I again went back in grief.

School staff came to our class and called out my name. He told me that I was being called in the principal's office. I went there. O God! CUTIE's parents were there, sitting opposite to the principal. I understood everything, and with the due permission I went inside the principal's chamber.

"Yes he is the same guy." CUTIE's mother said pointing at me.

"You are a responsible person and also a good student then how can you do that?" Principal asked me.

"I didn't do anything !" I exclaimed.

"Do you have someone special among girls?" He questioned again.

I kept numb.

He urged me again to tell.

"I have a number of friends among girls and all are special." I explained.

"You please don't try to be over smart." Jacob said to me.

Mr. Jacob D'sauza was the founder member of our school along with principal and rajnikant.

"I don't. Sir!"

"Give me your number." Rajnikant said.

I gave it to him and then they matched the number and called, but luckily or say fortunately no one picked up the call. He gets annoyed and leaves the place.

"Why did you call Tamannah yesterday?" asked the principal to me.

"Just to talk to her" I said.

"What type of talk?" He enquired just like any CID officer.

"Just the formal talk." I said.

"We all know what your intention is?" Jacob said.

"Do you know her? Do you really dreamt of marrying that girl?" He further added.

"Yes!!!" I reciprocated.

I don't know what to tell but, what I told was the fact.

"Son, you are misbehaving." Principal got a bit serious.

"please suspend him for a week." That was what Jacob told to the principal.

"He's a nice guy. He is studying here since his childhood and no one had ever complaint about him. He should be given at least one chance." Principal put forward her views.

"Please, I insist you to suspend him". Jacob tried to convince the Principal.

"Ok."

"You don't need to come to school for next three working days as you have been suspended from school on behalf of your misbehaving." Finally Principal narrated the result of our long argument.

Lastly, I was suspended.

I didn't got worried but wanted Tamannah mother to be relieved, if she would be with what Principal did then might be she would send her daughter to school the next day.

I didn't go to school the next day and thought not to go for a week although. They had suspended me for three days and I would suspend the class for three more days. During my suspension period I kept asking about Tamannah to my friends. Whether she attended the class daily or not? Was she fine?

I completely left the school for a week and attended class a week later. I saw her and she saw me back and we smiled looking at each other. We had to be more cautious than before. Seeing her the blood level in my body rises up.

Being caught doesn't mean that we had to stop what we did but, it means to be more cautious and judicious. After that whenever we get time and opportunity we went together to the restraunt and spend some time together their.

Our board exams were hardly two months to go. We all accelerated our study. It was 24th of January on which our juniors decided to give us a farewell party.

My CUTIE's birthday was some 5 days earlier. We decided to meet but she couldn't come out from home as the school was closed for class 10th students. I wanted to spend the day with her but couldn't.

On the day of her birthday she called me and asked me to come near her house. I was the person who won't let any opportunity to go and I grabbed it to see her. I went quickly near to her house. She again called me but it was an unknown number for me. I picked up and Shalini was on the other side.

All the girls had gathered at her home for the celebration of her birthday. Shalini gave her phone to Tamannah and then we talked. As soon as I reached there I could see the number of girls on the terrace along with Tamannah waving their hands towards me. I had already bought the gift for my CUTIE but couldn't give it. After a while of standing near her house I put my step back to home.

In the evening when we talked I showed her the urge to meet her. For the same we decided to meet right on the day of farewell. But not at the time of farewell rather before that. Farewell was t be organized from 10 in the morning and we decided to meet at 8 am.

On the day of farewell she called me to say that she had left for the restraunt, but at that time I had just awaken from my sleep. Without taking up a bath I rushed to meet her with the gift that I bought for her.

We reached the restraunt and spent the time together. I handed over the gift to her and lost ourselves in talking. Again our hands were interlocked in each other and her head was lying on my shoulder and my hand was around her shoulder.

After two hours we turned back for our school. She had to go for her friend's house just a flat away from school and from there, they all would go together so I dropped her there. As there was some time still left for the farewell to start so I rushed back to home. While leaving she asked me, if I would come? "Maybe!!" I responded. "Please come!" she requested and how would I deny her request. So, I assured her to come.

I reached home, took a quite bath and waited for the friends to come so that we could go together. A little late but they all arrived at my home.

We reached the school and upto then the farewell wasn't started. Might be all were waiting for us to come. I had been always very popular face in the school. As soon as we reached we were asked to sit on the chair. We all friends opted for the chair in the last row.

Just after we sat there, there was the announcement of the starting of the events. They announced that one by one, everyone would be called upon the stage and he would have to perform the task written on the paper, that we had to pick up from a bowl filled with tasks.

The first name they called was mine. I was the first one to be called. I picked up the paper from the bowl, unwind it and, I had to dance. I pleaded to sing rather than to dance but they all were a stubborn and forced me to dance.

I too had to do that as there was no chance to escape. I climbed up on the stage and a track from the movie "Rab ne bana di jodi" was played. A little while of dancing I went down the stage back to my chair.

The next one to be called was my CUTIE, Tamannah. Actually, everyone in the school knew about us. Everyone considered us to be made for each other. Some of the girls even crowned us as the best couple.

She was called and as expected she went front. She too picked up one paper and she had to do the mimicry of our science teacher, but apart from doing so, she rushed back to her seat very unexpectedly. We enjoyed thoroughly. All were being entertained and crowned by a nickname given by the juniors and I was crowned by "Mr. Cool."

A day to go, it was 14th of February we thought to meet up but it was much tougher for both of us. Our board exams were only 15 days later, it was the time for our last minute revision.

We couldn't meet as her father still had eyes on her where about so we decided to meet up the next day rather than meeting on the Valentine's Day. Sahil was my closest friend, closest from the heart and from the distance of the house too. He also resides in the same colony. I told him about our plan to meet up and told him to handle the situation if he met up with my mother as I had already told her about the extra- coaching classes to be attended with you.

It was 15th of February and we were to meet. She called me to inform that she had left for the restraunt. I also left for the same. I had a gift with me which I had to gift her for the Valentine's Day. We met in the restraunt. My eyes glowed seeing her. She always looked better than anyone. We hugged each other and the valentine kisses to follow next. We didn't have much time; I mean she didn't have much time to stay longer. But in that short span we talked a lot, kissed a lot, hugged a lot. It was the time for her to left and we both got up to leave.

I touched her face gently with both hands and then I moved ahead a little in front of her; we were getting closer, her eyes were much closer. She then closed her eyes and left herself in my arms. I bent her a little and kissed her on her forehead. She then opened her eyes and I told her to take care of herself.

We went out of the restraunt and then I dropped her near to her house. While we were about to leave from the restraunt we exchanged our gifts. I reached home happily, and saw my mom outside the gate waiting for me.

"Why are you late?" she questioned me as I reached near to her. I was really very late so she was a little tensed and worried for me. My mother had a specialty. If I was late even for five minutes than the usual time, then she would always wait for me standing outside the gate of the house, continuously scanning for me on the way to home.

I tried to explain her that there was much traffic on the road so I got late. She agreed and took me in for the snacks. I then asked my mom for the reason to stand there whenever I got even a bit late. O'er this she replied that, she is my mom and then she said,

"Leave it, you would never understand." We then got inside and had some snacks as I was so hungry. After the snacks I straight away went into my room and got busy in preparing for the board exams.

It was not more than 10 days left for our exams to begin and I got stuck with the very high fever. Studying in that condition was very difficult. I couldn't even stand in my own during that time.

Seeing me in that critical condition my mom called the doctor at home. With certain examinations and considering my symptoms he prescribed some tests to be done. It was hard to take me to the cab for further testing, but anyhow my parents managed.

A day later the reports were to be taken and my parents went to the doctor to get the report and certain suggestions from the doctor. Initially I was fed with saline. CUTIE called me, it was not easy for me to talk because of the facts that firstly I didn't have much energy to talk to her and secondly I didn't want to give any kind of tension to my CUTIE at the last moment of the exam.

I gathered all my energy and picked up the call. I didn't tell anything to her but anyhow she get to know that something went wrong with me. She kept asking to me if I was fine? I answered that, I was good and nothing happened to me, but she was someone who didn't let it go that easily. She kept on asking, technically not asking rather pleading to tell her the truth.

I didn't want my CUTIE to be in such a mess so I told her everything. As I told her she then started crying on the phone itself. I could easily listen her weeping, her whooping sound could clearly enter into my ears. Crying infront of me let me feel that someone had fired a bullet into my chest. For a moment, I wished and urged her to calm down and stop crying, but then I realised that she needed to be called with all my love to made her stop crying.

I then told her not to cry for me, I would be alright very soon but her sound instead of stopping got crumbled down and she started weeping too badly. I thought to be with her so that I could make her calm, wiping away her tears.

My repeated request and love made her feel better. She was sobbing. I too was in tears and wailing, but I managed to make myself calm otherwise she would have been broken and would burst again into tears. I just asked her not to bother much for me and just focus on her studies as the exams were too near. I also asked her to promise me not to weep again for me, but neither did she promise regarding that, nor did she stop crying. I couldn't continue myself to talk to her as I was under the supervision of my parents and sisters. Before disconnecting the call I had made her much calm and almost stopped her from crying. She asked me that, when would I be free again to talk to her? I promised her to call again whenever I get time. She wished me a good luck for my health and also prayed for my recovery. In the end she said "I LOVE YOU!!" I replied back as "I LOVE YOU TOO!!"

Continually she wept during the call whenever we talked. After four to five days I started recovering and this made my CUTIE calmer than before.

Actually I had infection in my blood and the medicine given showed its effect after certain days. I too wanted to get back to my previous condition to study, because in that situation I tried a lot to revise my subjects but not with much ease, but yeah I didn't lose my heart and tried my best in doing everything that I could.

I was recovering and so was she. It was all her love which made me recover so soon.

From the day I told her about my health, she only cried and prayed for me. She did everything for my good health. She was on fast every-day, after knowing about my bad health, and on that day itself, she put aside her books and just sat infront of the statues of God and started chanting their names and praying for me to heal me quickly from this bad health.

Exams were on the head and she didn't even care for it rather she did everything for me. She didn't study the text book but enchanted the 'mantras' the whole day. When I told her that I was healing and probably be fine after some days then only she looked towards the book and quit the fast.

I was too glad and proud to have her. I was fully determined to marry her and make her my wife and to lock her in my heart forever. She was the single piece on the earth and God had created her only for me. I love my CUTIE and love the way she was, so cute, so innocent, so shy, so understanding, so caring, so intelligent and more over that, so loving.

It was the first day of the exam, our centre was somewhat 12 kilometers' away from home. I was not fully well and even if I was, then too my mom would surely follow me to the centre, and she did. I took a book to revise in the car and my mom took everything along with her to pamper me. Two bottles of water, not less than 5 cans of juice, all the medicines, some chips and biscuits and everything else on which she could feed me, as, till then I wasn't allowed to take any solid food. In home I was only fed with juice, pulse and milk.

We reached the centre and made a quick revision. Students were asked to get inside the centre with the required stationary. I got inside and reached to my respective place as per the seating arrangements.

A while later many girls surrounded me asking for my health.

"Who told you about me?" I asked them.

"Who else other than Tamannah!!!!" they replied.

"When we were talking on the phone I asked her about you and suddenly she started crying. I asked her why to cry? Then she told me everything about your health. She was crying too much and anyhow I managed to calm her down." Explained Rishita.

"How are you now?" she added.

"Yeah, fine but will take some more time to heal." I said to them.

"Ok, best of luck for your exam and also good luck for your health and hope you to get well soon." Said Shalini.

We were busy writing our papers for complete three hours. After three hours we all got out and discussed about the papers with each other. No one ever did had said that his/her paper went bad. May be it is the human psychology.

Those who used to pass with grace or hardly manage to pass also bet to get more than 80 marks in the paper. They tried to psychologically win over other or either to have upper hand than others.

I too was not expecting anything less than 90. As I get out I saw my mom waiting and seeing me she smiled. As I reached to her she asked me about the paper and I told what I expected. I was given some juice to drink and then I had to take some medicine.

I knew it that ones I got out I couldn't be able to talk with CUTIE so I talked to her inside the center itself at the centre. She looked me carefully from toe to the head and then, she asked me about my health. I told her that, I was alright and was recovering at a faster rate. She further ordered me to do as doctors said and to take care of myself. I too replied softly that when she is here I need not fear and no need to care for myself. I tried to tease her.

She smiled gently and told me to shut up and said me to do as she said. I accepted her order and said, "As you wish Maam." Our whole month was destroyed by giving exam, no love, no meeting nothing. We never kept apart ourselves for such long time.

Exams were over and results were to be declared two months later, most probably in the last week of May. We didn't had anything to do other than calling each other.

We talked even more than ever before. Whenever we had time we made a call. During that time within 15 to 20 days we were always there in the restraunt to meet. Though it was not so easy for her but yet, she got the permission to come out in the name of market, just for me.

In these talking and meeting two months passed away and then in a day or two the results were to be declared. The date of declaration of results shifted everytime. It was the time when I had to left for Delhi to give certain exams. I reached there with my brother and his wife and halted there, at my sister's place. Before leaving for Delhi I told my CUTIE to return back soon and also not to call on my number.

I had given the exam, scheduled just a day after I reached Delhi. On the way to centre I got stuck in the traffic jam and then, reached there half an hour later than the start time of the exam. They allowed me to give the exam only after knowing the reason for being late. I quickly rushed inside and followed the staff member who was directing me to the class.

The paper was good, not too difficult, and I did it with much like recklessly and ruthlessly so quickly to compensate the time elapsed. I ended up leaving some questions untouched.

In the exam of two hours if you are late for half an hour you can't expect to attempt all the questions. In that time itself, you need to fill up all the formalities before you start writing on the answer sheet. My next exam was week later.

My father didn't wanted me to qualify that and even not to attend for that paper. He asked me to leave that exam and return back soon.

Actually I too didn't want to appear for that exam. We cancelled our returning tickets which we had already registered and then got a new one of two days later inorder to return back.

Next morning I woke up by the voice of my sister, who wanted me to talk to the person on the phone. She had phone with her and she handed it to me saying that my father wanted to talk to me.

"Hello!" I spoke rubbing my eyes.

"Hello! How are you son?" Father said from the other side.

"Too good! And you?"

"I too am fine, anyway congratulation dear!"

I was shocked. "For what?"

"Don't you know?"

"What father? I was sleeping just now"

"Your results are declared just now and you have scored high!"

"Thank You! Papa"

"Your mother wants to have some words with you."

"Ok! Give her."

"Hello! Son, may you live long." My mother wished me.

"I will but you too, must."

"You have made your mom too happy Son!"

Then I had some talks with my mother and before disconnecting the call she blessed me with everything and as much as she could.

The story doesn't end up here, much more calls of many other to follow the whole day with congratulations.

Finally I reached home town and the first thing I did was to call my CUTIE. Actually I gave her a missed call on her number just to inform her that I was back. As I informed her to arrive after a week before I left for Delhi, so I just gave her the missed call so that no one else could pick the call.

Some half an hour later she called me back and was too happy to knew about my return. When she asked me the reason for arriving early, I just gave her the reason of my dad's wish. She further asked me about my exam and I told the incident happened to me.

I congratulated her without even knowing her marks, percentage and everything, but the thing I knew was that, she had passed the board. She congratulated me back. We didn't have talked for many days and our love was coming out of our soul and every part of the body, so we continually stuck to the mobile.

Now the most crucial time arrived for us to choose which way to go. I opted for the science and she, for the commerce.

She went to the best school in the city mend for girls and I too chose the best of my knowledge.

During our classes in school we bunked our school in every ten days and spend the whole day together in the restraunt.

It was the day of 'Raksha-bandhan' and at the same day we opted to meet. She called me and told that she could come only in the evening for some time. I agreed.

In the evening we reached the restraunt for our meeting. Everyone working in that restraunt knew us very well, as we were the regular customer their. We reached the restraunt and grabbed the opportunity to hug. We were having the sweet talk and suddenly we see the rain drops rolling down to earth from the glasses of the restraunt, it was raining. We were enjoying the romantic evening. But the rain didn't stopped and it was going too late for CUTIE.

It was raining too heavily, only water could be seen everywhere. It was more than our expected time to stay together. She needed to reach home in time but rain was a hurdle at the time. We were waiting for the rain to stop. After a while rain stopped, and then, she asked me to leave. I did the same. She told me not to drop her near to her place as it was already late and my mom would also be in a hurry to see me but how could I left her alone. I insisted her I would reach home anytime, it doesn't matter but I wouldn't let you go alone.

We get out of restraunt and sit in the cab. It has rained too heavily that, everywhere we could see was water, the driver dropped us on the main road nearby her house and from thereon we had to take a short walk.

We walked a little straight and then we saw water upto the level of our half of our leg. We stopped there but due to lack of any other choice we decided to go into it.

We were walking-cum-swimming on road. We were just half a minute away from her house. While walking or swimming we had our hand interlocked in each other. We clutched it tightly.

I would never forget that day in my entire life. Our clothes were all wet below the thigh. I dropped her near to her house and again went for a quick swimming. I reached home safely but couldn't avoid the water to splash on my body.

Our love life was on the right track and all because of my cute, charming, gorgeous darling. She was CUTIE for me and I was SWEETU for her. She had nicknamed me SWEETU and whenever we talk she called me SWEETU everytime.

She had changed my life from dilapidated to a life on a high note. It was vengeance for me. My life was exhausted without her. Whenever I talk to her or be with her, her too gentle demeanour made me actually believe that, how special I was for her. When I saw her, she let me pinned down. I continuously kept seeing her without a blink of my eyes.

I had always been too notorious in class and everywhere. Every guys used to call me as the 'Dada Bhai' before she entered in my life. I did sneering at people very oftenly. Those who ignored my words I tormented them.

She entered into my life and everything changed. My all previous deeds was toppled down and now I venom my own habit that I used to have earlier. It was new version of mine, everybody could easily get it.

She was having some health problem with her. Every after a day or too she had to face and cope up with headache, fever, and pain in her throat. Doctor after examining, prescribed some tests and when the reports were shown to the doctor, he declared that, she was having 'Thyroid'. Doctor prescribed some medicines which should be taken everyday in the morning by her, an hour before she ate anything.

She took the medicine and followed the rules for few days but then she forgot to take it the other day. I repeatedly requested her not to let it go in any case but she wasn't habituated yet. If this would remain for long time then she would have to suffer extreme situation and her thyroid would enlarge. I then thought to message her daily to remind her regarding the medicine.

Since then I use to message her on her cell to have the medicine. And it showed it's fruitful result. She used to have her medicine everyday and whenever she would forget to take that, then my message flashed on her cell would remind her soon.

Being in a relationship is something really great and with the girl like my CUTIE, it is something above than the heaven, it would obviously make you over-whelming. She was just wonderful, thought-evoking. I was in relationship. I was really committed not in my words but also with my work and soul and I accepted it gleefully. I wasn't single and didn't want to be either. Her phone call meant everything to me and it always made me waiting to see my phone vibrating. Reading the short messages that she sent to me proved to be hilarious and refreshing. It knocked down every single stress and strain. I was fully charged and was completely dependent on her for my happiness.

'It's more than 15 days, we haven't met for a single time. I needed to meet you SWEETU. I need to spend the time in your lap, need to rest my head on your shoulder. I need to kiss you. I need to hug you.'

'Me too CUTIE. I myself want to talk to you but you yourself told me, making me feel so good. Everytime I asked you to come but today it is really great to listen these words from you.'

Initially in the beginning she was so prude to even talk to me, but slowly getting the required ability and pried apart her prudeness and now today she was speaking those words which, I was very much eager to listen from her.

We decided a date to meet. My phone was beeping while talking to CUTIE. I put it infront of my eyes and it was my grandfather on the waiting line. I told Tamannah that, my grandfather was on line and told her that I would call her back.

I disconnected the CUTIE's call without much delay and answered to my grandfather's call.

"Hey! Grandpa, how are you?" I asked as soon as I picked up the call.

"Me fine son and you?" My grandpa replied.

"Me too fine. How did you call today on my cell!!!" I gently asked him.

"Yes son, I had been trying a number of times but couldn't reach out to your mom's number." Grandpa said.

"Is your mother present at home?" He added.

"Yes, wait. I'll let her talk to you."

I reached out to mom and handed her the phone. She then talked to grandpa for some minutes and then asked me to take back my cell.

I went to take back my phone and when I was about to leave, she told me that there was a marriage in our village and we must have to go.

'Yes, mom you should go if grandpa had asked.'

'Not only me! but you too had to come as the wish of your grandpa. Being the eldest son in our family, grandpa wants you too to come.'

I don't know why the elder people want their eldest child to be there with them in every function. The situation had excruciated me. I was committed to meet in the due date with my love and a day before the date I had to go. I was in a total mess.

The total situation created prancing and provoking me. I tried to let my mom understood but she wasn't ready to listen. I decided to talk to my father without telling to my mom.

"Hello!" said Father.

"How are you?" I asked.

"Fine! And you and your mom?"

"Both are fine!!" I said.

"When are you coming back to home?" I asked.

"Why are you asking me this question?" He asked me rather than answering.

"Don't you know about the marriage?" I further asked him.

"Yes-Yes, I know." He then replied.

"Father actually I also had to go, but I don't wish to go on the day with mom because I am having my classes those days and I would come three days later on the day before the marriage. I wished you to come and take mom to the village." I pleaded my father.

"Is it necessary to attend the class son?" He questioned me.

"Yes, father. I had always been a regular student, punctual to school. I had never missed any of the classes out of my wish. So, I need to attend."

"Ok, I am coming two days later and will take your mom with me."

"Ok, bye!" I bid him bye.

Father arrived and took my mom with him to attend the marriage. Next day we were to meet and these things done by me was just to not let slip the opportunity to meet my CUTIE.

On the scheduled timing we met at the same restraunt. My heart kept bouncing whenever I saw her. Half a litre of blood in my body got increased seeing her. I had my life with me.

She hugged me and I felt like to be in heaven. She kissed me and I found myself to be hypnotized in her love.

We altogether had a refreshing day. It was much needed for us. Seeing her, my all the problem vanishes.

She wasn't anyone but the most important for me. We talked much and shared much of our thoughts, but most loving was the eye contact and then the cute smile from her side.

The time flew away very quickly when I was with her and it was time to left for the home. We paid the bill and then left. As usual I kissed her on her forehead before leaving. We had our hands in hands throughout the time we were together, even while traveling in the cab, she held my hand tightly.

We left the cab and moved towards her house in the colony. On the path we had some talks. Just a few steps before her house we bid goodbye to each other and then moved to our home.

While I was on the way back to my home, a person with his squalid condition approached me. He ordered me to stop. I did the same. I never knew him. He asked me that who I was and I too asked him the same. He told me that the girl with whom I was walking was his sister. "Which brother? I know her real brother." He then replied that, she was her cousin sister.

He further asked me to stop talking to her and thinking about her. It was hard for me to endure what he said. I replied him back that whatever he could do, can do but I was never going to leave my CUTIE, never ever.

He bellowed on me not to do it again and I shrieked on him back. He seemed to be out of anger.

Squabble between us gets onto high and got worsened and worsened.

When it was hard to handle for him, he then strikes. He punched me on my chest. He hit me with his immense power he had, though I survived.

I gave him back his dues with much more power and intensity but, on his face.

Oh! He was bleeding. May be some veins of his nose got burst out and he was bleeding, it was bleeding from his nose.

Pucker on his face could easily be seen. He was seeing me as if what I had done. I had imbued his heart with terror.

I didn't stop myself from hitting him although he was bleeding. I shrilled a punch into his stomach and he shrieked out suddenly with pain.

I was busy in giving him back what he reaped. Suddenly someone held my hands and restricted me from my action sequel. If they wouldn't have held my hand I would have pulverized him.

What the fucking hell? They were all excruciating me. They all hit me everywhere they could. The man who held my hand wasn't alone but with three more people of his type for the backup. Maybe the person whom I did hit, was either the friend or the relative of them.

Seeing the backup for his rescue, he felt more courage within him and struck me recklessly and ruthlessly. I was done by then and it was time for them all to be precarious to me. They might have the propensity in their gene.

I was left helpless. Anything may go wrong with me, I won't bother, but nothing should affect my face. I cared for it much more than any, but they all bullshit didn't seem to care for it. I was bleeding from everywhere, from nose, mouth, cuts on my face. My eyes got blackened. My every bolt was loosened and still they continued to hit me. They dragged me and threw me to the wall nearby. I was forced to hit against the wall and my head witnessed the harsh strike ever.

I held the head with both of my hand. It was too heavy then, that I could be burst out anytime due to immense pain. They jumped on me as if I was their prowl.

Except for the one among them, no one even knew the reason for the action scene. I was much like any villain of any romantic film but how could I make them understand that I was the hero!!

They didn't show any mercy on me and constantly kept hitting me brutally. Upto then many more people have gathered there around the scene. They tried to intervene and after a little difficulty everything stopped.

Till then, everyone among them had given me not less than twenty-five punches. My condition was dilapidated. I was feeling little unconscious. I was bleeding heavily from nose and mouth. My inner skin of mouth and jaws also witnessed the cut.

I was the punching bag for them. My whole body was crying from the pain and all I was bearing just for my love.

Someone from the crowd offered me his hanky but I nodded. They asked me to left the place but instead I stood still and saw around to all five of them.

I scanned their image in my mind. Then turned to move. I was bumped Lion by then. While leaving I threatened them to be ready for the consequence.

Just a meter from then, I saw the tap of water. I get around their and tried to wash my face off blood. The more water I poured on face, the more blood dipped down. As I touched my face with hand, I felt the intolerable pain. I then sprinkled the water on face without even touching the face. It took me long tome to wash off face.

I then soaked the water droplet with my own hanky. Even though I washed, my hanky get colored. I reached home and thank God, no one was present. All my family except CUTIE went to village. There was no one from whom I could hide my wound.

Reaching home I first of all made a call to a friend of mine, actually not a friend but, we knew each other very well. He respected me very much. He was the don of our whole locality.

I called him and told everything. He felt too angry and asked me to come out and let him knew the face of that guy. I made him calm. Luckily I knew the one among them. I told him about the guy I knew and he promised me to take my revenge with the guy tomorrow itself. I hung-off the phone then.

I looked myself in the mirror as soon as I entered the house. I was badly hurt. It was evening by then, but I could easily find the dark spot beneath my eyes. My face was little swollen. There was a cut mark on my face and my mouth which I could spot through the mirror.

I went to have a bath to feel little lighter. I applied liquid antiseptic on the wound inorder to heal it and prevent from infection.

I talked to my CUTIE and when she got to know that something had happened to me she kept insisting and pleading to tell her, but I thought that, I shouldn't tell her on my own, instead I told her that she would get to know automatically within a day only.

It was neither any shyness nor the ignominy to tell anything to her, rather it was my worry for her. I knew it very well that, if ever I told her, by my own then she would ask me the whole sequence and the every place on my body where I was hit. Then what would I tell her that, there wasn't a single place on my body that remained untouched by those culprits.

And if she would ask me about the bleeding then it would further increase her grief and then she surely cry. She would then experience the huge pain, so I didn't tell anything to her.

The only thing that made me much worried was that I had to attend the marriage the next day itself and then, if anyone there would notice me then, I would have to make a false reason for my condition.

I engulf a medicine to get some relief from the pain otherwise I wouldn't have slept that night due to pain.

Next day, Tamannah called me and as soon as I picked up the call she asked me that, if I was beaten up by someone? I replied positively.

'How dare he touch you? I will kill him if I get him. Who is he to do with us?' She showed her anger for him and care for me.

'Be calm darling, nothing happened to me. By the way, how did you come to know about this?'

'That culprit came to my place and said everything to my mumma. Thank God, father wasn't there at that time. After then mumma asked me when he was gone that, if I knew the boy with whom that culprit quarrelled. I just replied that, I didn't have any idea about what and whom was he talking.'

'Do you know him? Was he your relative?' I asked with curiosity.

'Yeah! We have relation and somehow he is my cousin, a real fucking moron. I will surely tear him off if I get him.'

She was more ferocious than a lion.

'Darling did he hurt you badly?' She further asked me.

'No, I am fine darling, no need to worry for me.'

'Hey, Hey, Hey!! Please stop crying darling, don't cry please. I am really fine. See I am talking to you just like before.' I tried to make her calm then.

'No, they hurt you. They beat you very harshly. You went through this just because of me.'

'No darling, please don't cry. Don't blame yourself for that.'

'Please tell me. Are you alright? Please dear.'

'Yes, ofcourse dear, I am much fine.'

I forgot the pain and was happy that she felt my pain and stood by my side. She was with me and ready to tackle with any situation that went through me.

I made her understood and stopped her from further crying. She always told me to take care of myself as I didn't belong to only myself and asked me to have the medicine.

If she would be there with me at that time, I wouldn't have felt any pain, rather I would have slept in her lap.

My eyes were wet till then. It was tears of happiness that she was with me. She loved me from the core of her heart. It was more than any other happiness for me. I forgot the pain as my happiness over powered the grief. I was happier than before to have her. She made my life and it was only because of her that I was happy instead of crying in that situation. I didn't want to be seen weak infront of her, else she would be broken.

I was healing by then, the swollen face was getting to normal and very soon I would be fine as before, I hoped. The dark circles under my eyes were getting healed. The next day arrived and I had to left for my village that day.

Before leaving the home I talked to her and she was more nervous than me. She kept telling me to medicate well. She asked me about my wellness, wound and my pain. I answered her everything she wanted to know and assured her that I would medicate myself very well and would take care of myself.

I was very thankful that I had reached there in evening when it was about to be dark and then no one noticed my wound or the spots. It meant that I had one more night to heal my wounds and make it better. I took the medicine and applied the antiseptic on my face.

My grandpa was too happy to see me there a day before the marriage. Whenever I went to the village he asked me to sit with him and we talked for hours and had the dinner together. He was much happy to have me around him.

Next day when I got up, I immediately rushed towards the mirror to see my face. It was healing at the faster rate, the swelling on my face had completely vanished but the pain was still there with me. I didn't bother about the pain as no one would see it. The dark circles around the eye weren't gone but it wasn't much of worry as I would tell people that it would have happened due to less sleep.

I could be seen well, but internally I was totally dismantled. I couldn't even eat any salty or spicy things. I was much cautious not to be seen worried.

As soon as the marriage ended I went to my home town the very next day itself, leaving behind my entire family by giving the false reason to attend the classes.

I was healing and so was my wound. We almost forgot that incident and met many times after that with ease. In every ten days we were sure to meet and apart from one or two, I dropped her near to her house without any fear to be getting beaten up again.

We were having good time together. Days were passing and we also passed the eleventh class and got promoted to the twelfth. I love her and love everything of my CUTIE. I love her cute little face, her charming smile, her innocence, her attitude, her infinite care for me, and I love her 'Karva-Chauth' which she kept every year for me. I never expected this from anyone but she did everything for me, always made me feel much special and too lucky to have her.

My CUTIE I Love You, you are so special for me.

I could bear every pain for the smile on her face.

It was the month of December, so chilling and windy weather. We were having late night talk on cell phone. We almost talked till 2:00 am. Whenever we met out in the restraunt we had very less time for us and we wondered if, we could have a longer date. Everytime we talk about the short duration of meeting but neither could she do anything nor could I.

We were talking làte in the night. She told me that her parents were going to Delhi for the check-up in AIIMS. It wasn't new to my ears as they did it in every two to three months. Next day when her parents went to Delhi, we had a late night talk and I asked her to meet and we could spend more time together as her parents weren't there in the city.

'No, I can't. I can only come out to meet when my parents are there in the city. My grand parents will never allow me to go anywhere in the absence of my parents.'

'Ok! You have your own reason. I thought that it would be a good day for us to meet and spend some longer time together, but anyway not to think much for it, we can't do anything new.'

'SWEETU we can, if you are ready. My parents aren't in the city and if you can come to my place at night then, what do you say?'

'In night!! But what if someone saw us together? How could I? Grandparents are already with you, they will surely know it. we can't keep ourselves hidden from them.'

'No SWEETU, nothing will happen. My grandparents are an early goer to the bed and the whole locking and unlocking of the doors and the windows is done by me or under my supervision. If you will come then, I will keep the keys with me and will open the gate for you.'

'Is it possible darling? I mean, isn't there any chance to be caught by your grandparents? If my parents wake up before I return then what?'

'Darling nothing will happen! I promise that, my grandparents and my younger brother will never know it and if you come then we will have the whole night before us to spend together.'

'You coming na SWEETU??'

'May be!!' I replied her.

We were fully prepared to meet in the night. I knew that, it was winter and my parents would be fast asleep by 10 and on the way too there wouldn't be much people to encounter me.

I told my mom that I had to attend the marriage of my friend's sister. My mom asked me the day when to attend, I told her the present day.

'You never told me about it before but today itself you said. When you wish to go and at what time will you return back?'

'Mom, I forgot to tell and I will go anytime in the night. My friend will come to pick me up and probably I won't be able to return back at night rather, I will be back in the morning.'

Listening to all she first of all tried to pry me apart from the marriage. I insisted her but she wasn't ready to move. It took a lot of time to convince her.

When we talked in the evening I gave her the green signal to be available before her.

In the night around 10 she called me to tell that I could go there as her grandparents were asleep. They had been sleeping from the past one hour.

'I am coming to your home. When I will reach the famous temple nearby your house, I will give you the missed call and then you open the door for me.'

I left my home after 10 pm at night and then started to go straight to her house. I was feeling much cold. My whole body was vibrating. I was shivering with cold. My heart was throbbing very fast. I reach to the temple and then called her. She picked up the call and I told her to open the door. I went ahead and just a while later her house could be seen. I went closer and closer and soon as she saw me she opened the gate and let me in. I was more conscious than a thief. She locked the door slowly so that no sound could reach to her guardian.

She turned and started to move to her room. I simply followed her without uttering a word. We went inside a room and bolted it from inside. It was her parents room and she got the chance to sleep whenever her parents went away. She hugged me as I entered. She felt so happy to have me there with her. I clutched her tightly and went on for few minutes.

We were all alone and no one was there to disturb us. We could spend time together. Kiss followed the hug. We sat on the bed and started talking, and after sometime she went to switch off the light so that, her family would think that she had slept. We continued our talk and love. We were holding each others hand. It was cold and so we were sitting so close to each other that our body felt the touch of each other's.

We kept talking and we caress our body and kissed each other more than anything. One and a half hour passed away so soon, but still we had much to talk.

My hands were around her shoulder and her head was resting on my shoulder. Suddenly we felt something, we were too close to each other, and the caress on the body aroused a sensation in our body. We can feel each others heart beat and it was pumping at the higher rate than the normal. Her breathe was getting heavier.

We saw each other without any conversation as if whole words were being explained through our eyes. We got much closer to each other. We turned a little towards each other. Her eyes were closed and head was down. I got closer to her and we started kissing each other.

We held each other so tightly. I caressed every part of her body. She was ready to give me everything. I took out her clothes and she was left only in her undergarments for which I took no time to threw it away from her body. I threw out every clothes from my body too.

We were left with our natural clothes. She was feeling so shy that she didn't even saw me once at that time. I reached closer to her and made her lie down on the bed. I was more than ready. I reached between her and slide my manhood into her womanhood. She moaned. I was into her. We were one body with two souls. When we were on the midway, she looked at me with love in her eyes. She held my face and kissed me for too long. I kept sliding myself into her. She was clawing deeply on my back and asked me to hold her very tightly.

Her clawingness would have hurt me any other time. But at that time I felt it great and it excited me too. I did it with more energy, then after a while we both reached our destination. We were done then, and were looking into each others eyes. I could see a sense of satisfaction in her eyes. We kept ourselves in the same position for some more time and then apart us from each other. We were cloth less whole night. We made love two more times before I left her home early in the morning. I reached my place very early before her grandfather woke up.

She had fully devoted herself to me. The whole day, incident of night ran into my mind. It made me felt in heaven. She had fully frilled my life. She had faith and trust on me and I would never crush it, neither I would let her go anywhere away from my eyes. I had sex with her and I would make her my wife anyhow, I thought.

Three more months left for our board exam. We studied as much as we could. We studied upto 5:00 am in the morning and in between whenever we got bored of studies we had a talk on phone but it never lasted more than 15 minutes. I did apply for some competitive exams too so I had to focus on study more. Due to much busy schedule of mine I wasn't able to give her more time as before, but she never complained.

She understood and had faith on me. she completely supported me.

Our board exams were over and I had to give the competitive exam for which I had applied.

Exam of IIT was scheduled in the very first week of the April. I studied day and night. On the scheduled day I went to appear in the exam. It happens in two shifts. All the main papers like physics, chemistry and math had to be given twice. In the first half I went to appear and started doing the paper. My physics and chemistry was stronger than the math. I started from physics.

First half was really good one for me. I hoped the next half too, would be same for me. I revised some formulas outside the gate of the centre. I had some juice, then, we all got inside again to appear for the second half.

I took the paper and started going through it thoroughly. It was much difficult than the previous one. I tried to do it but, it proved to be a little harder than expected. Although I did it with the patience and knowledge I had, but it wasn't as good as the previous one, still I hoped to get qualified.

Someday later our AIEEE exam too was going to be held. I prepared myself for it. Everytime my CUTIE wished me good luck for the exam. I was so confident to qualify this exam as, I was completely prepared for it.

It was the day for the exam and as expected, my CUTIE wished me good luck before I left. I reached to my centre in the city and got in. After getting the answer sheet and the question paper I started solving it. It was easier for me and I did it with much ease.

I firstly tick the answer on the question paper only and thought to do on the answer sheet later. When I was completely done, I took the answer sheet and started to fill the bubbles.

I was busy in filling the bubbles and suddenly my eyes went to the next bubble which I had to fill, I was filling the right bubble but on the wrong serial number.

I looked back quickly to the previous one. Oh My God!! I had filled the wrong bubble. The option 'C 'of question number 11 was to be darkened but, I filled the option 'C' of question 12th and till question number 18, I did the same. I filled the right bubble but of the wrong question. I was about to cry but couldn't.

I was damn idiot. I kept abusing myself. I ended up screwing myself.

Many more exams to go on and in almost every exam I did exceptionally well.

Two months passed by then and our results of 12th exam was declared. I passed the exam with the first class, but it was not what I expected or what my family expected from me. I talked to my dad and told him about the result, he congratulated me and suggested me not to think about what happened or if, I didn't achieved my expectations and asked me to do better in the future.

I was waiting for my competitive results. I had a lot of hope from there.

I got a call from VIT that, I got selected in their engineering program and also they asked me to be present for the counseling. Getting a call from such a reputed institute and also to hear about getting selected filled my heart with joy. I told my mom about getting selected and she was also happy but was waiting for my IIT result.

AIEEE results were declared and I knew the result much before it was declared. Although I qualified but it wasn't enough for any NITs.

I made my mom aware about the result and she seemed to be disturbed. She had a hope from me and I faded her hope.

I was left six marks short to be selected for IITs and my mom after then seemed to have no hope from me. She wasn't talking to me directly. I was left alone with my CUTIE.

My father told me to wait for the result of IITs and NITs and also some other one's too, rather than going for any counseling. Waiting for some results snatched my opportunity to get myself counseled in many reputed institute. Everyday I got news from some institute that, I got selected there. I got selected in four common entrance tests, three private institute exam, two marine institutes and two aero-space institute. But my mom doesn't count on that. She wanted nothing else than IITs or NITs and I failed to get it for her.

No one asked me by what marks I was left short, but everyone asked me about not getting selected for that. My father was a gentle man, he never tried to force anything to me, but my mom was not ready to listen. The one I qualified didn't stand by my side. I didn't get myself enrolled for counseling in many institutes.

I was in a great dilemma. Only CUTIE understood my pain and stood with me in every situation. I was too much depressed. I quit eating. I quit talking to anyone. I kept myself locked in a room. I only ate a little due to my CUTIE.

She kept asking me about my food. My happiness was completely gone.

Why people don't understand their child. Why they judge their child by the selection in IITs, NITs and AIIMS, and why not by their ability and capability.

I was also the one affected by such thought. Smile on my face had completely disappeared.

She called me and I talked to her but I neither smiled even a single time nor did I try to do so. I cried everytime and so was my CUTIE. I never wanted to cry before her but, I did and due to me, she too cried everytime. She urged me, pleaded me to forget all and asked me to get out of the situation and be happy but I wasn't.

I kept myself locked and cried in that room. In the evening time only, I opened the door and got me out of that place and then I straight went away towards the ghat and sat there idly for hours. I didn't even talk to my mom.

When CUTIE asked me to meet, I got there to meet her. I felt good to see her, had her, but my sadness wasn't too small to forget. Many a time I didn't have any money with me and then she met me and gave me her pocket money.

I didn't want it but she insisted me to take. I didn't have any of my pocket money during that period and when we met then, she paid the bills. She always tried to make me happy. But I was completely broken from inside. Smile never rode through my face those days. I was quite numb and was lost. My CUTIE always tried me to overcome the sorrow. She tried her level best to do so and did everything for me.

My depression situation lasted for completely two months and in those days, I never talked to anyone. The only one I talked with, was CUTIE and while talking to her, I cried almost everytime, but she never let my moral down during that period.

During my depression period I was left alone in the dark but she proved herself as the bright edge to me. Without her I wouldn't have lived. She tried to let me see the ray of hope by her brightness.

I went to ghat regularly in every evening to spend my time there. Whenever we met she was sure to pay the bill and also to give me her pocket money.

I was hopeless as almost every counseling was closed and I would end up my life fucking up myself. I thought many times to end up my life but then, she kept me alive. I was hopeless to do anything, hopeless to get any good college.

Later when my parents realized, they also tried to get me out of that mess but it wasn't so easy for them as I was in real depression which could be healed only when I would get enrolled to any reputed college. Every counseling ended up just the last one was left. I applied for it online after regular insisting by my CUTIE. I registered for counseling but didn't have any hope to be selected for a good college.

A week later my mom got a phone call from a reputed institute of Pune about my selection there. She asked me to open up the door as she had good news for me. I opened up hesitatingly and then she gave the news that I was selected and I was really happy.

I called my CUTIE and told her about my selection in such a reputed institute. She was so happy to know that.

I counted the day when to go but really sad for getting enrolled in a college too far from my beloved. Days passing quickly and the time arrived when I have to say good bye.

I meet my love last time before going. We were sad for my departure and nervous for what to talk. We spend the time together and whole time our hands were interlocked in each other. When leaving, I kissed on her forehead and we left keeping our eyes wet and with the untold promise which we made in our heart never to lose each other

I went to Pune for the further studies and she too was doing law from a central university. Everyday we talk and show love on the cell phone. We are in contact with each other.

Both of us are waiting for tour studies to complete and then we will get marry very soon. We are leading a happy love life and whenever we had time, we meet each other in the same restraunt.

During vacations we met a lot. Though she is in the home town now and I am too far from her, still there is no any sense of inconvenience between us. We both are loyal and faithful to each other. Hope to get married soon.

Love You Tamannah, Love You till the end of my life.

EPILOGUE

Being so much apart hurt us a lot, whenever getting time we meet in our hometown. Our bonding grew stronger and stronger despite of being too far physically.

Having a long distance relation is really a hefty job but continuously maintaining it without any argument and fight is somewhat more hefty but we are having a doctorate degree in our relation and it goes on smoothly and romanticly.

Putting aside our ego and having full faith, our relation rises on the higher note.

Most important was that we are together and always thought to be.

WHEN IMAGINATION TOOK THE FORM OF WORDS, RESULTED IN A BOOK.

Printed in the United States
By Bookmasters